RED MILL CANY

MW00942511

REFINERS FIRE

By Brian Voigt

RED MILL CANYON SERIES: BOOK TWO

Copyright © 2018 by Brian Voigt

All rights reserved. No part of this book may be reproduced without the permission of Brian Voigt. The scanning, uploading, and/or distribution of this book via the Internet or by any other means without the permission of the author and publisher is illegal and punishable by law. Please purchase only authorized electronic editions and avoid electronic piracy of copyrighted materials.

Your respect and support for the author's rights are appreciated.

Edited by: Nancy Voigt, Jerry Ott, Carol Bench and Glenn Bennett
Interior and Exterior Fonts: Times New Roman, Copperplate Gothic, Adorn Serif, Ariel, Eterea Pro, Copperplate Gothic Bold
Interior Photos and Images: Shawn King, Brian Voigt, iStockphoto,
Cover Concept: Brian Voigt
Cover Design: Brian Voigt
Exterior Photos: Tom the Photographer/Unsplash, Brian Voigt, Christopher Burns/Unsplash

Scripture quotations taken from The Holy Bible, New International Version® NIV® Copyright © 1973, 1978, 1984, 2011 by Biblica, Inc.™ Used by permission. All rights reserved worldwide.

This is a work of fiction. All of the characters, names, incidents, organizations, dialogue and businesses in this novel are either the products of the author's imagination or are used fictitiously.

Connect with the author online at:
Website: BrianVoigt.com

Table of contents

DEDICATION

For Rick Carus

You built foundations for Christ and touched many lives. I was lucky to be a part of your first youth group right out of seminary. You taught me living for Christ is about helping others. You also taught me to appreciate music and the power of the group and its ability to change lives. I experienced my first *Miracle of God* under your leadership. Most of all, you taught me to take my appreciation for Christ and His work on the cross to others and share Him.

Today, as I ponder your recent death, I look at life in retrospect and realize just how short it really is. You, more than any other person, set my life on a foundation of ministry to children. Thanks! This book is dedicated to you and those who had the foresight forty years ago to hire you at Christ United Presbyterian Church in Phoenix, AZ. May God's blessings continue to rain down on those whose lives you touched.

ACKNOWLEDGEMENTS

My friend Michael Brown and I sat on the porch of Starbucks over three years ago, discussing the fact Winters Edge, once the manuscript was finished, actually had what it took to build into a series. It was a thrilling experience to define the geography of this future series while outlining plans for the first six books, all individual stories within a much bigger story and purpose for a series.

The first trilogy of Red Mill Canyon, Winters Edge, Refiners Fire, and Autumns Child, was written with a purpose, to bring the reader in book four to the realization that all along, the first three books were weaving a much bigger story which begins to fully unfold in the second trilogy. Michael had everything to do with assisting me in that process. Thanks Mike!

I'm grateful for our local Starbucks staff who encourage me constantly as a writer. Thanks also to my wife and daughters who are a source of encouragement to me as they listen.

I pray you will also be blessed by this series!

PROLOGUE

Red Mill Canyon, located in the Eastern Sierras near the High Desert basin in California, is an ongoing series about Red Mill Ranch and Rails End. In *Red Mill Book One: Winter's Edge*, Bill Simmons and his three daughters, Shawny, Crissy and Missy Simmons are recovering from the devastating death of his wife, Celia.

Grady, the manager of the Red Mill Ranch and Owners Association, begins dating Valerie Dobbins, the town surgeon of Rails End. Valerie becomes aware that dating a man who is running one of the largest ranches in the Meadowlands, and the initial rejection by his daughters, is more of a struggle than she was prepared for. The challenge of one of the harshest winters in years and their common love of adventure bring them together in the end.

Winter's Edge ends with Valerie's realization, in spite of their differences and the difficulties, this is the man who she wants to be with in the future. They have been courting for one year at the beginning of *Red Mill Canyon Book Two: Refiner's Fire*.

- 1 -

PROPOSALS

"…Shall we accept good from God, and not trouble?…." Job 1:10

Bill Simmons held onto his brown felt hat, as the soaring March winds blew hard across the North Rim. He sat in the saddle before the largest pine tree on the ridge, staring at the five names carved into the tree, Jimmy, Johnny, Cass, Mac and Billy. The weathered, fifty-one-year-old cowboy had tears in his eyes, remembering the moment which defined part of his childhood. Today, thirty-five years later, only four of the names carved on the old tree remained in Rails End. Mac, the son of Horace Grady, had ascended to leadership of the rail yards. Jimmy was now the town Sheriff and Johnny the owner of the Sierra Roadhouse. Cass … *well* … no one really knew what happened to Cass or where she was.

The tall trees swayed in their grandness like a symphony only the Creator could compose. The dirty, brown lapels on his lambskin-lined coat flapped in the wind, as he looked down on the ranch he had come to love in the last year.

To be honest, he had loved this beautiful canyon his whole life. Each ridge which stood tall above the large spread below held memories, memories of riding with his father and hunting with his grandfather. But actually living in Red Mill Canyon, and the turbulent first year it had brought, was now a blessing in Bill's mind. Today was a day unlike any of the others as he sat on the mustang which snorted and jostled under him, looking out over the valley in the upper region of the Sierras.

Grady Simmons, as he was known on the ranch, held his large hand in the pocket of his coat, turning the small, velvet covered box in his fingers as he considered the future. The thoughts about the future flooded his mind with questions. *"Where would this lead him? So much had changed in the last year!"*

This box he held in his hand was a new start. The pain of a long year-and-a-half of change was about to be flooded with a permanence that would bring a newfound joy and love. Looking down at the ranch, he could see Valerie from the distance as she walked in the field with Shawny, his oldest daughter. This week would be one year of courtship and a pending engagement.

He turned Rocket's reigns to the side and clicked his tongue. "Let's do it, boy!" He gave the horse a light kick with the heels of his boots as they started the descent down the path to the bottom. The cowboy enjoyed the view, the vivid colors of the green pines and the bright red hue of the earth, knowing Rocket would lead the way. The large mustang had been down this path a dozen times. With each opportunity a view between the tall trees allowed, he looked down on the two women as they slowly walked across the meadow behind his cabin.

The meadow was one of Valerie's personal joys. She remembered that day, the previous spring, when Grady had walked her across this meadow with its blooming flowers and wavy, Russian grass with the bright red stalks which swayed lightly in the wind. Though the grass was a light, brittle brown with winter's deadness now, no blooms filling the field, she touched the grass with the palms of her soft hands again in a girlish manner, listening to Shawny speak. He watched from high above them, smiling at the thought of that memory.

Shawny was a young woman she had come to love during the harsh winter. Grady's oldest daughter had been the one in his family who embraced her during the rough beginnings of a love affair with her father, which had grown stronger with each month. She knew it was just a matter of time and the relationship would be a permanent one, one that lasted for a lifetime! The issue had already been settled between them. She was simply waiting out the formalities. In the beginning it was Valerie who had drug her feet as she approached this friendship with a man who was twenty-one years older than her. Lately it was Grady who had been dragging his heels.

"I want you to be my maid of honor, Shawny," the thirty-year-old said as she watched for the girl's response.

She stopped short of a full step, looking up at Valerie with a smile on her face. "It will be the wrath of Missy if I do. She thinks our mother's turning over in her grave right now!"

She stopped and put her hand on the young woman's shoulder. "Shawny … I would never try to take the place of your mother. I realize Missy's your Daddy's little girl, but life gives us what God provides. I love your father. I just want to know I have your blessing. Missy will come along when she's ready."

"I want you both to be happy, Valerie." After a long hesitation, she said, "He *is* happy now. It reminds me of our days on the Acreage. He loved life there! After we moved into town, he lost a lot of the joy he had when I was a little girl. I love the fact he has that sense of adventure again."

After a moment of silence, she drew in a deep breath. "What color will I be wearing at the wedding?" she said with a large smile on her face.

Valerie turned and hugged her. "You don't know how much this means to me, Shawny!" The two women giggled their way back to the cabin as they talked with a newfound excitement about the plans for the wedding ceremony.

Douglas Thomas III was a man of precise calculation, a lawyer by trade with a family firm to protect. The president of the Red Mill Ranch Owners Association spent the winter fending off legal action against the ranch and its owners, as the news of the biggest scandal in the Meadows Region in thirty years hit hard, along with the first snow of the previous winter.

With the arrest of the ranch's employees, Darcy Jenkins and Joe Brine, and a member of the board's executive committee, Peggy Withers, the inevitable lawsuits followed. Just as Sheriff Jackson had warned, the end result of the entire scandal could mean lawsuits. The board could have weathered the actions of a few crooked employees, thanks to Grady's quick action and a thorough process on the part of the sheriff, Jim Jackson. But the involvement of a leading member of the board was something they couldn't dodge, regardless of Douglas Thomas' experience with these kinds of legal issues.

He knew an institution that was attacked from the outside could, in the long run, sell some assets, fall back on insurance, and ride out the storm with the help of the next ten year's profits. When the lawsuits from the owners themselves began to stoke the fire, the Association had become divided and was feeding on itself. As the long winter wore on, his own family became worried. The frankness of the conversation and concern for their law firm now hung in the air.

"Doug, I wish you would have given up that board seat when we asked you to a few years ago. You knew the place was taking a slide on the balance sheets for a long time now," his father reminded him. "Red Mill Canyon became a thing of the past for the entire family a decade ago. When was the last time you actually hunted up there, Dougy?"

The reserved man in the double-breasted suit remained quiet, looking out of the glass walls of the skyscraper, viewing the sprawling city that was Los Angeles from the tenth floor. He simply remained quiet till they all had their say.

Jennifer looked up at her brother with empathy. "Doug, I know you love Red Mill Canyon. We all do. Some of our most memorable Christmases were spent in those cabins. I love the fact you share that with your own kids, but it's time to be honest with yourself. We all knew there were problems for many years on that board. The ranch may still be making some profit, but the problems have been ongoing for twenty years. That's why Daddy pulled out of it a long time ago. Now our ties to this thing are dragging the firm down. Three more lawsuits were filed this month against us because you're the president of the Association board."

The Thomas family had made their decision. It was time to not only get out of Red Mill Canyon, but the owners needed to sell it, as well. Selling it would divest everyone of the problems that had rocked the Association and the lawsuits would stop. "Make it profitable for the owners to sell and they will do it, Doug," his sister persuaded. "It's time to set your personal feelings aside and get on with it!"

Grady sat on the log rail of Jed and Betsy Gentry's front porch, the largest staff cabin on the ranch and the place that had hosted his girlfriend during what had been a year of courtship, whenever she visited. The Gentry's house was the gathering place, a cabin with four rooms which had slowly been added onto over the thirty years they lived on the ranch.

Valerie leaned forward with her smaller arms around his neck and shoulders as she stood behind him, pressing her face against his cheek. She was enjoying a privilege she rarely had with this taller man. The two smiled, looking down on the antics of his three college age daughters who were speaking with Jonathon Harris and Jason Twibley.

"That Crissy can be a bit of a tease, Grady!" she laughed as they watched the girl swipe the boy's new white, reed cowboy hat, tossing it to her sisters and making the young man run back and forth. Jason finally stepped in, rescuing it from the girls.

The father of three watched his daughters. "Jonathon ain't the brightest bulb on the ranch, Val."

She pulled her head away from his and said, "Ain't, Grady?

Really? You're talking about Jonathon's lack of intelligence and you use the word ain't. I think we need to have you visit a few of Miss Sharon's classes over at the schoolhouse when she teaches the kids their English lessons."

"I know you're a doctor, Val Gal, but there's more to brains than the words you use. The boy's a hard worker, I'll give you that much, but sometimes that noggin of his misfires."

"You know, I seem to remember him doing a really good job of getting this ranch back in order when it was buried under five feet of snow, while you took care of me after the storm!"

He nodded his head in a bouncing manner, from side-to-side, as if to say, "I know you're talkin' but I'm just shinin' it on."

She smiled and slid her face next to his, embracing him tightly, biting the edge of his ear. He pulled his head back with an annoyed look. After a short stare, he took the opportunity of her playfulness to give her a kiss on the lips. The young surgeon stared back at him with a look of affection. It was a probing look which said more with her eyes than she knew she should say with her mouth. Spring Break was almost over, and it was time for the girls to return to Lamont College. She wanted to make an announcement before they left.

He drew in a deep, slow breath as he looked at her with a backward tilt of his head and said, "Let's take a ride in the Polaris. I have something I want to show you." He flipped his legs over the railing of the porch, and she took his hand as they walked to the dirt road, jumping into the small all-terrain vehicle.

Grady brought the bright-red buggy to a slowing halt as they neared the top of the narrow logging road, before it turned along the crest line of the Sierra Highway. The road was dubbed 'The Kings Highway,' named after the regal and huge sequoia trees, the largest pine trees on the entire continent. They sat in the leather, cushioned seats for a minute to enjoy the highest view from the road, above the entire Red Mill Ranch. He loved this bend in the road, a small pullout where the rim road took a sharp turn as it passed a ravine, which ascended up high beyond the pavement.

After a few minutes, he jumped from the small vehicle and walked around to help her from the seat. The two walked up the ravine path, a trail which was maintained for hiking by the ranch staff for sunny days like today. As she looked around, admiring the wide-open spaces which were layered with a cushion of pine needles between the trees, he took a sudden detour off the path as they held hands, helping her up the steep side of the ravine to what was known as simply *The Rock*.

The couple climbed carefully up the sides of the hill, traipsing over large, jutting boulders the size of a car. After a few minutes of climbing, they stood at the top of the hill on the peak of a behemoth boulder. He sat down on the rock and coaxed her to sit in front of him, so he could hold her smaller body tightly in his large arms as they looked out on Red Mill Canyon. They snuggled tightly in the light breeze that blew over the hill. He lifted the velvet box from his suede coat pocket.

He took her hands into his own as he wrapped his arms around her and shifted the pretty box from his hands to hers, waiting till she realized he was pushing something into her palm. The man wasn't much for fanfare.

She looked down at the box with a sudden furrow of her brow and stared at it for a moment. She lifted her head and looked out over the valley, as the tears welled up in her eyes, making him wait for the emotion to pass. The moment she had been waiting to share with this rugged man had finally arrived.

She laid her head back against his chest and lifted the box up so he could see it when she opened it. She pressed the lid up and looked at the small ring with the large diamond that sparkled in the sunlight. She wiped the tears from her face and ran her forefinger over the stone, pulling the ring from the box.

Her fiancé took the ring and gently slid it on her finger, and she held her hand up so they both could look at it. "I didn't want to make a show of it in front of the others, Val. I just wanted it to be you and me, right here on this rock. My granddaddy proposed to my Nani here. It seemed like the right place to do it."

After another long pause, she scooted her legs over one of his and laid her head against his chest. He looked down at her face that ran with tears, kissing her. He held her in silence as they listened to the wind for a half-hour.

She finally mustered the courage to ask. "Why did you take so long to give me the ring? I was worried you were having second thoughts. Was it because of Missy?"

"No, Val," he sighed. "Missy has some things to work out in her heart. The poor girl didn't even know her mother was dead until a week after the accident. She got a bad shake with that whole thing. Missy's gonna be Missy, no matter the path my life takes." And then he asked, "Do you know what day today is, Val?"

She lifted her head, staring up at him with a puzzled look. "I'm thinking Saturday's probably not the answer you're looking for here." Then it suddenly hit her! She gently pushed his cheek back with her palm. "You old sentimental cowboy! Today's exactly a year from the day I came up to see you on the ranch the first time!"

"Today's the anniversary of the first time I held your hand!" He looked down with a big grin on his face.

"I have to tell you Bill Simmons, that almost backfired in your face. Any other man and I would have said, 'No!' If it wasn't for having such an adventure that day, and the fact you were rebounding from a terrible six months, I would have run from you as fast as I could. I just didn't want to hurt your feelings, Cowboy. I still can't believe you grabbed my hand like that and started holding it while we were talking."

After a moment of silence, she looked up at him again, "But I *am* glad you did it, Bill. I just don't think I would have even considered dating you. That was the furthest thing from my mind. And *yes*, I was there to hold the hand of a Christian brother who I thought was still hurting!"

After a short pause, she said with a smile, "You played that moment well, Bill. And I have to tell you, what you said to me that day caused me to stare at the ceiling as I laid in bed that night. I didn't know what to think of you after that!"

- 2 -

DIAMONDS AND DEPRESSION

Old Jed was in high spirits, spending the afternoon sitting out by the big smoker which bordered the pavilion. He was smoking a load of ribs and chicken for the feast which was to take place on the ranch that evening. Springtide had arrived, the day of celebration which the staff enjoyed every year when the snow was nearly melted, and the small, green plants began to poke through the soil. The first Sunday of spring, toward the end of March, was reserved for the huge festival. The entire staff brought their families up to the ranch for a barbeque and dance which was unrivalled by any other event that took place on the ranch.

Springtide was Jed's day to bask in the glory, watching the crowd savor the meat as it was pulled from the smoker, which billowed with a cloud of pure, white aroma. This was the day he taught the younger cowboys on the ranch the finer points of western living, as they helped him prepare the large, black tube for a smoke run. Wood had to be piled, the firebox lit and the meat rubbed down with the salty-sweet, red seasoning which he prepared from his secret recipe. The older man spent the entire afternoon rotating the meat, as it slowly cooked.

Valerie sat on the porch with Grady and Betsy, watching him teach the younger cowboys his skill. "He sure makes a fanfare of it, doesn't he?" she mused, as she and Betsy watched from the large, cabin porch.

"Yes, he does, Valerie! He looks forward to this day all year. This is the equivalent of Christmas to him. He loves that old smoker at the pavilion. He and a few of the men welded it themselves back when old man Stevens was in charge of the ranch. That was a great time for all of us up here! A lot of construction went into this place during those years. Springtide Celebration is about memories for Jed. Stevens always said, as a man gets on in age, memories is all he has to pass on. Now *Jed*'s the old man on the ranch. He takes that saying very seriously."

Grady leaned toward Betsy and smiled, "He's a great mentor. He knows his place up here and does his job well! I wish we had a few more men like him."

She rocked in her large, wooden rocker, doing her knitting, as she replied, "Don't sell yourself short, Grady! The boys respect you after running that bunch off the ranch. These days, I figure you could tell 'em to jump from 'The Rock' at the top of the canyon and they would do it."

Valerie and Grady looked at each other with a grin, and he nodded his head hard toward Betsy with an emphatic gesture. She stood from the wicker couch and sat in Jed's rocker. "Grady took me up to 'The Rock' yesterday," and held her hand out in front of her.

Betsy lifted her head to squint through her bifocals and exclaimed with a cry of joy the two had never seen from this woman they cared about. The two ladies jumped from their chairs. She grabbed her, giving her a hug, and ogled the large diamond. "You did well, you old Cowboy," walking over to Grady and giving him a big hug. As she pulled her head back, she grabbed his face with both hands. "It sure took you long enough! I was about to give up on you. I told Jed the other day it was time for him to take you out in that cow pasture and get a lesson or two from those bulls."

Jed walked up the steps to the porch, stomping the red dirt from his boots as he leaned against a post, smiling. Valerie held her hand out to him with tears in her eyes and he chuckled. "Oh, I've seen it, young lady! He must have shown it to Donavan and me about a dozen times this last month. Betsy's been asking for two weeks why the calendar in the kitchen had a red star on yesterday's date. Grady and I put it there just to get her asking questions."

She walked over to Jed and gave his cheek a soft shove with her hand and kissed him. "You two are a couple of codgers. You know that?"

"So, when's the big announcement?" he asked. "Seems to me Springtide's the perfect day to tell the others!"

"We're waiting for the dinner tonight to make the announcement," she said with a sparkle in her eyes. "I just wanted Betsy to know first. I showed Shawny last night. That's why I invited her over and we shared the bed in the guest room. It was our girls' night out. I don't think I can keep her quiet about it if we wait another day."

She grabbed Valerie again and they did a little dance. She took her in the house to pull out their own wedding photos and share them with her.

Jed sat on the wicker couch with Grady, waiting till the ladies were gone. "There's been an awful lot of meetings taking place up at the hall the last few days, Boss. The board has had the door locked all day."

He stared off at the cow pasture with a look of concern. "It hasn't missed my attention. I thought about going up there to see what all the commotion is about. I decided to hold my water a bit longer before I stick my nose in the middle of it. I plan to invite Doug Thomas over for a drink tonight and have a talk with him. I don't like being left out of meetings between the board members. The thing which concerns me the most is some of the others were here yesterday. It's not just the board members. Ron Givers and Simeon Smith were both in there yesterday. That group on the board won't make a move on anything important without Givers' input. He pulls an awful lot of weight when he's in the room."

"Ya' know, Grady ... Stevens didn't like the control the Givers and Smith families had when he was here, either. He told me one night, as we sat on this very porch, those two families played a big part in the purchase of this Canyon. He also said your Granddaddy owned a part of this place up here as well, when the Association took it over."

He looked at Jed with a solid stare for a few seconds, thinking this conversation out before going any deeper with it. "I'm gonna tell you about that, Jed. But you need to understand it's a real sore subject with my relatives, so we don't talk about it. When my Uncle Hank found out I was taking the job as the ranch manager ... well ... let's just say he was pretty angry about it. The whole land purchase with the Association wasn't exactly on the up and up when it happened. They tried to cut my grandfather out of his ownership of the property when it was sold to the Association. If it wasn't for how Jamison set up the land trust, they might have gotten away with it. He was a real smart man, that Jamison was. He liked my Granddaddy a lot."

He shifted in his seat to face Jed, sitting back slightly. "My grandfather did a lot of things for Jamison when the Mill operated. Provided a lot of services, it wasn't just hunting. I have memories of them hanging out together when I was just a small kid. Jamison paid my grandfather half cash, and half land. Put the whole arrangement in a trust that would be passed on through the deed to the property. He knew the timber contracts with the Forest Service would play out after about forty years. He was the sole owner to the mill property, even though the rights to the timber were granted by the government. He owned the canyon from rim-to-rim up here."

"By the time Red Mill closed down, Jamison had transferred ownership of a third of the canyon to my grandfather. The Smiths and the Givers each owned a third of the land, as well. They had ties to the milling business the old logger operated. I don't exactly understand how it all came down. What I do know is, when they tried to foreclose on Jamison, they weren't aware my family owned a large part of this valley. It sort of turned into a range war for a time. They stopped my family from running our cattle up here. Even tried blocking the roads off. It all ended up in court more than once. They eventually had to face up to the fact they couldn't break the trust he created for my grandfather. But ... they did succeed in stopping us from using the land for a while!"

Jed's forehead turned to deep furrows and he narrowed his eyes. "So, Grady, are you telling me you own a third of this canyon?"

"No. The whole thing was settled when the Givers and the Smiths agreed to buy the Acreage my family owns down in the Meadowlands. Grandfather turned his part of the deed over to them in a trade. We actually ended up with twice the land than we had up here when the negotiating was over, and the dust settled. But … we could no longer use Red Mill Canyon for hunting or running our cattle. My grandfather raised three sons up here on this land. It was a pretty big blow to him. I never heard a good thing come out of my father's mouth about those two families. My uncle was actually wounded in a little skirmish with their families. It turned into a bit of a gun fight one day. That's why he has that gimp arm of his."

"So, how do those two families still have control if the Association bought the land?"

"Well, as near as I can figure out, they sold a majority of the voting interest to the Association, but they still have a large enough interest in each family to control an important vote if a portion of the Association vote with them."

Jed sat and thought this out for a long spell. He turned and asked, "So, tell me this. If there was so much animosity between your family and theirs, how did you ever get hired up here last year?"

Grady looked at him with a smile. "I've been asking myself that question ever since they agreed to hire me, Jed. I just wanted to be here because it was the land I loved and played on as a kid. I wasn't a part of all that legal wrangling when I was just a pup. But I do love being here. I suppose they just figured the past was the past. None of us who are alive today in any of the families were a part of the fight that took place, with the exception of my uncle and Simeon Smith. My Uncle Hank's still alive. And now he won't talk to me. He calls me a traitor. My cousins just laugh about the old man's antics. They were pretty unhappy with me when the whole thing about the swimming hole came out last year, though. Everyone can use the roads up here now. We just never told anyone about the swimming hole. It's just over the fence line a ways. And my personal family's the only one who kept Sonrisa up and swam in it. My cousins just got their pride hurt a bit because everyone in the family knew it was my Granddaddy's favorite place."

Jed stood up and said, "History ... don't ya' just love it! I better go check on the meat. It's about time to start getting the pavilion ready."

Valerie looked up into Grady's eyes as they danced that evening, her heart all a flutter through the long, drawn-out evening of festivities. The staff, the board and their families ate barbeque and made a fun time of it. As the evening progressed, though, Grady became more unsettled as he looked on while the board members sat in pairs, here and there around the pavilion, quietly talking. None of them seemed to be enjoying the dance.

She finally coaxed him up to the stage and he took the mic as they stood together before the crowd, announcing their official engagement. She showed off the ring to the group of ladies who rushed the front of the pavilion. All of the men shook his hand with a hearty round of congratulations. And from that point on, it was a real celebration.

He looked across the decorated, dining area with concern. It was obvious to him his younger daughters didn't take the news that well. Missy angrily sat at a table with her arms crossed, staring her father down. Crissy was entirely absent from the event. Crissy's absence was a surprise. He thought his second daughter was fine with their relationship at this point.

The evening began to draw down after a final hour of slow dances. While the band played, Douglas Thomas III drew closer to the stage and decided it was time to take the mic. Each of the men took their wife or girlfriend and they cleared the dance floor to take a seat. It was tradition that the president of the board gave a closing talk. Usually, it was a talk about the successes of the year, an opportunity to give out thanks from the board, and point out those in the crowd who deserved special recognition.

This year turned out to be different!

He looked for a way to begin but started to get emotional as he faced the silent crowd. As the pressure built with all eyes on him, he struggled to speak. After a long, awkward pause, Jennifer Thomas stood and walked to the mic. The young professional recounted the long love their family had for Red Mill, a place they all enjoyed as they grew up. She then made it clear to the group assembled before her, all good things must, eventually, come to an end. "The Association has decided to close the ranching operations and sell the hunting preserve. Things will be final by summer's end."

The murmur turned from a low sound of voices to a louder cry of surprise which spread across the gathering of people. Valerie watched Grady and Jed as the announcement hit them like a ton of bricks. The tall cowboy slumped down on the bench seat he was standing near, looking down at the cement floor. Voices began to demand an answer, so Jennifer told them the truth. "The board has been fending off lawsuits because of what Darcy, Joe and Peggy did to the ranch. The costs would be devastating to many owners if the situation continued the way it's been going. Yesterday, a majority of shareholders in the Association voted to sell. We're not a business corporation. The owners are an association. The laws in this state don't protect us from these kinds of lawsuits. A lot of us own family businesses. We have to protect our businesses." Jennifer gathered her brother, without taking any questions, and they walked away.

Grady spent the next hour talking to employees without having any answers. When it ended, the couple sat on the porch alongside Jed and Betsy in total silence, as Shawny, Crissy and Missy looked on. No one said a word. It was simply over. The only sound coming from the porch was the squeak of the floorboards under Jed's rocking chair as he held a tumbler of Wild Turkey in his hands.

Crissy surveyed the depressed gathering and still wasn't sure what had happened. She had snuck away during the dance and was the last to arrive on the porch. She knew enough to understand something terrible took place while she was gone. She remained silent for the moment. She was avoiding any questions which might come her way about their sudden disappearance and where they had been during the dance.

The young woman sat on the floor of the deck near the steps and pulled her knees together tight, wrapping her arms around them. She laid the side of her face against her knees with a worried look as she watched Jonathon Harris with the crowd of cowboys who were still gathered in the pavilion. As he listened to the cowboys talking, he glanced back at her several times. She finally turned her head the other way and watched her father as he sat on the wicker couch with Valerie.

The moment didn't miss Betsy's attention. She watched Crissy quietly close her eyes and turn her face into her knees. Her glaring eyes gazed across the dirt road to the pavilion, watching as Jonathon turned away, avoiding her intent stare. Betsy lifted her knitting from the porch table and sat back knitting. Her quiet eyes scanned the entire group on the porch to see if anyone else had noticed.

- 3 -

BROODING

The following Saturday, Valerie watched from a distance with the women in Betsy's front room. They planned out the wedding with all the excitement a future bride would want from the other ladies who were present. The thirty-year-old surgeon was privately worried about her future husband, trying to make the best of the moment, while being inwardly divided in light of the terrible news about the closing of the ranch. She sat in the couch chair in the corner of the paneled living room, smiling back at Betsy, Shawny and Crissy, but her eyes were really tracking Grady through the big window. He was slowly walking across the fenced-in cow pasture which sprawled out in front of the large, cabin house.

He bent his tall frame and squatted in the middle of the pasture, taking a long blade of grass into his teeth. He looked out across the ranch in each direction. She wasn't sure if he was angry, depressed or simply reliving memories in his head about the years he had spent in Red Mill Canyon. One thing she knew for sure, Grady was deep in thought and was distancing himself from everyone on this sunny morning. When a person wanted to be alone, the cow pasture was where they went. The others on the ranch knew when they saw it to give the person their privacy.

Donavan stood beside the greasy, maintenance table which sat in front of the maintenance shop, his stained hands on his hips as he stared off in the distance. Jed was working at the table on a pump from the old pumphouse which stood in the corner of the cow pasture. "What do you think's going on in his head, Jed? He's been out there for two hours now!"

He glanced up at him from the corner of his eye with an annoyed look, as he tried to pry a bolt off the pump. "If I know Grady the way I think I do, he's hatching a plan, Donny Boy. We've all had a week to chew on the fact we'll be out of a job soon. Grady's still chewin'. Just give him his space right now till he's ready to talk. His family's history runs deep up here."

At noon, Jed and Donavan went to the old man's cabin for lunch. All week, the noon meal had become a group luncheon since Valerie and the girls were spending so much time in Red Mill Canyon lately. As they entered the dining room, Jed piped up and said, "Is he still brooding out there?"

Valerie stood by the window. "No, Jed. Something's up! I'm not quite sure what's going on, but he and Shawny have spent several hours in the office. It's unusual for the two of them to be gone together for so long."

Betsy called for Missy and Crissy to help put the serving dishes on the table and get the place settings ready. They sat down at the large, slab table and began passing the mid-day supper, a full course of fried chicken, mashed potatoes, green beans and biscuits. Betsy loved cooking for a crowd. She missed being able to do that. Donavan was smart enough to know if he hung around Jed's house lately, he would eat well.

The group sat around the table chatting during the meal. Grady pushed the door open, and he and Shawny took their places at the dinner table, filling their plates in silence. The entire table was quiet as they watched the two catch up on eating lunch.

After a few minutes, he looked up. "Love your cookin', Betsy. You need to give Val your fried chicken recipe."

"Don't need to, Grady. She cooked the chicken herself!"

Valerie watched his sudden look of shock. "She's been learning a lot about cooking these days. Been helping me out in the kitchen, lately. It's time you pulled your head out of that cow pasture and took notice of what's going on around here."

Her fiancé smiled up at her. "I'm impressed, Val! Have you been able to get that family secret from her for the country bread? Now that's a keeper if you can squeeze it out of her!"

Jed looked on for a minute, deciding it was time to get some things out in the open. "You wanna' tell us all what it is that's taken so much of your time lately? You've been brooding about that announcement since Monday. Let it out, Cowboy! You wouldn't be in the office with Shawny all morning if something wasn't up."

He finished chewing and threw his cloth napkin on the table, sitting back in his chair. "Shawny and I have been discussing a plan. I figure it's time for all of us to take control of our destiny. How would you like to be able to stay on the ranch and grow old here ... umm ..." he looked up and smiled, "*older* here? You too, Donny."

Jed folded his arms and the whole table sat in silence as they all looked at he and Shawny. "Does this have anything to do with recapturing your family legacy, Cowboy?"

"You bet it does, Old Man. It just might be possible to end up owning this entire valley *and* the Acreage down below. Having both of those spreads would give us everything we need to run a real good operation, one which pays some real money. And I'm not just talking about my family. I'm talking about you and Donavan, as well. It takes three, strong leaders to run the kind of operation I'm thinking of. If we own the ranch, the possibilities are endless. I'm talking about ranching, hunting, horseback riding. They're all a profit center. And the ranch out on the Acreage is just close enough to town to make a rodeo arena work on Friday nights."

Shawny engaged the conversation with an excited look, "I'm graduating in a few months. My degree's in business with an emphasis on ag management. I used to help my mom do the accounting when we lived on the Acreage. I can run the business end of it, which leaves you all to do what you do best, running the ranch."

"There's gonna be other offers!" Jed said. "You can bet the asking price will be pretty steep if they succeeded in convincing the Givers and Smiths to agree to sell. This idea of yours won't be a walk in the park, Cowboy." Jed looked on through his glasses with a backward tilt of his head, waiting for a reply.

"I have some assets, including the operation out on the Acreage. They can all be collateral for a loan, Jed. We both think it's doable. The two of us spent the morning going over the last ten years for Red Mill Ranch and the Acreage on the accounting books. Projected profits will also help to secure a loan."

"A big loan!" Betsy admonished.

"Exactly!" Grady intoned, causing her to a double-take, realizing he missed her point entirely.

Donavan watched the sudden exchange of eyes, "And you think the future profits would actually float the kind of loan we would need to do this, as well as pay for salaries?"

"And then some!" Shawny said. "There's more than enough profit between the two properties. The cattle operation down on the Acreage has been contracted out for several years now. If we take it over again, it increases the profits pretty significantly. Daddy contracted the farming operation to the Jimenez farm when we moved off the Acreage. There's more than enough area on the farm to provide alfalfa and hay for both ranches. Even if we had to continue buying from Delrosa, we'd be making enough money to do it."

Jed asked, "And how will Delrosa feel about that. Do you know how far back that hay purchase agreement goes?"

"I'm aware of it." Grady stated. "I'll give them time to adjust. We'll probably keep doing business with them, just not out on the Acreage. But I don't want to start selling hay from the Acreage and push out some of the suppliers in the meadowlands. We'll plant enough for what we need down in the Acreage in the beginning."

Valerie asked, "Is rodeo really that big around here to justify an arena as a profit center?"

The entire table turned into a hive of laughter and Shawny said, "You bet it is! If we put an arena on the Acreage, it could draw people in from both sides of the Sierra's. Definitely from the Meadowlands area and the Desert Basin. We used to have a good arena, but it shut down awhile back when the Shelbys sold their ranch. It's not something you make a good living on, but it provides a little money if you already have a ranching operation. And the town loves it."

Valerie asked, "People will drive all the way up here to do that?"

Everyone started shaking their heads. "On the Acreage, Val Gal. But, if we put in some shops for the tourists up here and start renting out cabins, we could hold an annual rodeo and it could become a big thing. Do you know how many families participate in Gymkhana in this state? It's a huge sport."

Shawny said, "Think of it like an amusement park, Valerie. Maybe it's not a huge profit center, but it would make enough money for one of us to bring in a wage. We have the land and the livestock, and we're already in the high-risk category for insurance so that won't change much. It's just a matter of putting in the arena. And it's a weekend venue so it doesn't take much to run it on the side."

Valerie rolled her eyes and said, "I wouldn't have a clue. I'm a Scottish, city girl from Philadelphia, remember?"

Grady sat back and folded his arms. "Well, if this all works out in our favor, you'll be a Scottish girl from Philadelphia who owns two ranches *and* a horse of your own. You'll be the talk of the town with those relatives of yours back in Glasgow, now won't you? They already think you drive a horse and buggy to work since you got mixed up with all of us on the ranch."

As the group started laughing, Betsy stood and said, "Don't pay any attention to them, Val. Why don't you and I get the dessert served and let the dreamers keep dreaming?"

Grady picked up a piece of chicken and started eating, signaling he was done with the conversation for now.

BRIAN VOIGT

30

- 4 -

WEDDING ARRANGEMENTS

For five weeks, Valerie had spent weekends up in Red Mill Canyon, other than a few Saturday morning shifts she had to work at the Meadows Clinic. Grady and Jed had discussed, for several months, the need to provide an outreach in the Canyon area for the employees and locals who lived around the Canyon. Red Mill Ranch had an old church which was mothballed years ago. The men had spent long hours in prayer through the winter months asking the Lord if this was the right thing to do.

As spring came on, they felt God was leading them to re-start the church. Springtide had been the place they made that announcement, and for six weeks Valerie had helped Grady, Jed and Betsy launch the ministry and begin refurbishing the church. Each Sunday became an opportunity to hold worship in a building which was slowly improving.

As the April calendar was spinning off days at a rapid pace and the end of the month neared, the two knew they needed to make arrangements for the wedding. They decided this Sunday would be spent with the congregation in Rails End, to plan for that.

She sat on the hood of the large truck which was parked in the driveway of her house on Rose Lane and the two talked, as he stood between her feet in his black suit with cowboy tails. He leaned into the hood beside the large cab of the Super Duty with his arms around her waist. "Give me a kiss, Grady," she said as she looked into his face, teasingly, with a cock of her head.

He brushed her comment off and moved his own head to the side to look down the street toward Reverend Spicer's place. She moved her head with his, back and forth, purposely blocking his view, forcing him to look her in the eyes in a teasing manner to let him know she wanted this moment as she smiled at him.

She kissed him on the lips, and he pulled back. "I thought you were the one who was so concerned about the neighbors seeing my truck in your driveway awhile back. Now you're acting like a heifer in heat. What's with you lately?"

She smiled with a coy look saying, *"Mmmooooo!"* and kissed him anyway. "I told you I didn't want your truck in my driveway during the night and giving my neighbors the wrong impression. I didn't say anything about a kiss in the driveway, Cowboy. Besides, all the neighbors know we're engaged."

He drew in a long breath and kissed her for a minute. They could hear the Sunday morning belfries begin to ring from different areas of the city. She said, "I just love the sound of the bells on Sunday morning, don't you?"

"Girl, you got it bad right now with this happy, happy thing of yours! I think I better get you to church before you forget you're the town surgeon with that stiff, reserved attitude of yours. Last year it was like pulling teeth just to get you to hold my hand, Val." She laughed and pushed her man back, sliding off the hood, waiting for him to open the door for her.

As they both climbed into the truck, she slid over to his side as he shut his door and took his face in her hands, kissing him again. "Let me have my day, Bill. Today we meet with Rick and the pastor to plan the wedding. I know you've been through this before, but it's my first time. I've waited for this day my whole life. Just be my man today and be nice about it."

When the couple walked into church, Mrs. Spicer led the waiting group of ladies over to her with anticipation on their faces. As they approached her, Valerie held out her hand to display the engagement ring. They all swarmed her, giving her hugs as they walked off in a group toward the sanctuary.

Rick Seavey walked up to the grinning man as Grady watched

the whole scene play out in front of him. "Well, she isn't hiding the relationship anymore, is she?" slapping him on the back. "Congratulations, my friend." He hugged him.

"She's pretty happy right now. She was all over me this morning. It's been a while for me, I guess. So, we're on for lunch?"

"I wouldn't miss it for the world, Bill. I'm really proud of you. She put you through the ringer last year. She sure took her time about it. Come on and let's go worship the Lord together!"

After the service ended, the couple discussed lunch plans with Rick and the Pastor. As he began to head for the door, she suggested they go to the Cottage. "I haven't been there for a long time, Bill."

"I already called Johnny Jackson and let him know we needed reservations. Today's their Sunday brunch and his brother Jimmy's gonna be there also."

She hesitated for a few seconds and nodded with a pensive smile. "Okay. Let's go to the Roadhouse."

As the four entered the restaurant, he looked across the room and his eyes focused on Jason Twibley standing at the salad bar. He smiled and lifted his tan, beaver-skin hat with a nod at the young, ranch hand. Jason froze, holding his plate of food, unsure what to do.

Felicia, Jason's girlfriend, turned and realized Grady was staring at them and exclaimed, "Holy crap, Jason! I thought you said they were going to the Cottage!" After a long hesitation, as Jason stared like a deer in the head lights, she nudged him and said, "Smile and just nod your head and get back to the table. Don't just stand there looking stupid!" He waved with a fainthearted smile, and she gave Grady a broad grin and a wave with all the hospitality of a southern woman. The two quickly walked to the private booth at the back of the kitchen.

Johnny and Jimmy Jackson greeted the newly engaged couple

with a bevy of congratulations. Johnny walked them to the large table in the corner of the main, dining room. Then he headed straight through the kitchen to the private family booth in back, giving Crissy Simmons a shake of his head. "I don't like this, Girl! Your Daddy's like a brother to me. You know that! Don't ask me to do this again without him knowing you're in town."

After a hearty brunch, the four talked out the date and agreed on late September for the wedding ceremony. It would be a harvest wedding! Valerie looked up and said, "We'd like to have the ceremony in the meadow up at the ranch, Don. I love the meadow, and it gets its second bloom as the weather cools down in September. We can hold the dinner in the pavilion. If the weather turns bad, we can use the hall. It has a big kitchen."

Rick was hesitant. "I'm going to need a flat area. I don't do to well on rough soil after the accident in the engine house. It's the one thing I've never seemed to be able to master. The legs just don't work so well these days."

"I'll have the boys clear the area in the meadow and roll down the dirt. I'll make sure it's good for you, Rick. You're one of the few men in town I would want as my best man."

As the group talked, Jason Twibley walked up to the table, shaking his hand really hard. "I just wanted to tell you both how excited Felicia and I are about the news of your engagement, Grady!" As he spoke, Valerie looked toward the door while Jason blocked his view. In that moment, she watched, with a barely discernable shake of her head, as Jonathon and Crissy dashed for the door in a quick flash and ducked out of the restaurant, before her father could see her.

She looked up with a composed smile to conveyed to Jason her displeasure of hiding the fact Crissy was in town from her father. She was very aware, when the truth came out, it would unleash a devastating storm.

The following morning, Valerie quickly paced down the white corridor of the Meadows Reginal Clinic in her green scrubs and entered the lobby. She breathed in a deep breath and walked forward to Crissy. "You don't have to sit out here. You're family now. You can just go to my office in the future." Crissy stood, as she approached her, giving her future stepmother a hug. "Let's go in my office. We have to talk."

The surgeon sat the girl down in the fancy, leather seat in front of her desk. She sat in the chair next to her, taking her hand. After a long hesitation, she went straight to the point and didn't beat around the bush. She quietly stated, "The test came out positive." She waited for the twenty-one-year-old to absorb the bad news.

Crissy looked down for a moment and leaned forward putting her elbows on her knees, with her hands folded, in the cowgirl manner she had seen all three of the Simmons girls do many times. She looked off to the corner of the office with a look of shame and a quivering face. The tears began to flow as she started crying.

Valerie took the coed's hand and looked down, unsure what to do. She had been in this position so many times in the past, and it was always a hard moment. But she was at a loss for words now, knowing Crissy was her fiancé's daughter, and they were discussing her future grandchild.

"Legally, Crissy, I can't tell you what to do about this. But as your future stepmother, I can tell you you were brought up as a child of God. You need to do the right thing here. I'm not going to hide this from your dad if you don't. If he finds out about this and knows I knew … well … I'm not going to damage my future relationship with that kind of thing. Privacy laws don't extend to my being a family member and I'm not going to lie for you if you make the wrong decision."

The two sat quietly for a long minute and she asked, "Have you talked to Jonathon at all? You knew long before you came to the clinic you were pregnant. *I knew* before you came here you were pregnant. Men aren't so smart about women's issues, but Shawny told me about you being sick in the mornings. It was obvious to me. I think Betsy knows, also. I'm not sure, but she's been around enough years to know what was going on with the two of you during Springtide."

She looked up with tears streaming from her eyes and began bawling. She moved her chair closer and hugged the girl as she cried. "I tried to tell him. I mean, I dropped some pretty heavy hints about it."

Valerie let out an exasperated sigh. "You have to be straight out with the man. He won't understand subtle hints. Men aren't that way. Do you want me to be there with you when you tell him, or do you want to do it yourself?"

She looked up as Valerie handed her a tissue. "No … I need to do this alone, but I don't know what he's going to say."

She lifted the girl's chin with her hand. "Look girl, it takes two to make a baby. He's just as responsible for this as you are. Go tell him and get it over with. Today!" She looked off with a faint-hearted laugh as she muttered, "And I'll go hide your dad's shot gun."

She took her hands and prayed over the girl, asking God to give her courage and help her through the next two months. After they prayed, she said, "I'll get you on the bus back to Lamont tonight. Your Dad doesn't even know you're in town right now. The last he saw, you were climbing on the bus with your sisters after Spring Break. You're not going to be able to hide this much longer. I can tell you're already starting to show."

- 5 -

EXPANSIONS

On Monday, Bill Simmons sat in the large, meeting room of the Grady Corporate offices talking with Rick Seavey and Dan Edwards, the switching yard foreman. They were laughing about old times and the many stories they all remembered from working in the switching yards together. He had spent thirty years of his career with the Corporation, working from a yardman up the ladder to a corporate executive, before leaving the company after Celia's death to take the position on the ranch. As much as he hated the corporate job at the top, he did love being in this place when the Winter Committee met to have meetings. The huge, paneled room had a table that seated twenty which was cut from redwood when the Red Mill and Timber operations were still running. Leather executive chairs circled the table, and the cherry-stained paneling was adorned with large pictures of running horses and old locomotives.

Rails End was the railroad terminus for the Sierras in the Meadows Region. Though the committee was formed many years earlier to coordinate winter needs among the companies which surrounded the Meadowlands, they also met for other reasons when a problem had to be solved.

As the three men chatted, drinking their coffee, they could hear loud voices in the office next door. Mac Grady yelled from his office, **"Bureaucrats and environmentalists!"** Although Mac wasn't the oldest of the Grady children, he'd been the one to latch on to the family business harder than his other siblings. When Horace Grady became too old to work, Mac was the one who ascended to leadership and the family inheritance had come with it.

Mac had started alongside Grady in the switching yards when they were young men. Their families had been close as children. In the years that followed, their lives and families had become intertwined. Grady liked him. They had always seen eye-to-eye on what was best for both the corporation, and Rails End itself. The CEO was a generous man who had honored his father's agreements with the organizations in town. Mac had worked hard to make sure the transition of power in the corporation was seamless, as his father grew older.

"We have given the whole Meadows valley plenty of meetings to work this thing out. We offered three different plans. They're just being a bunch of selfish idiots! Don't they realize the growth in this valley wouldn't be here if it wasn't for the yard operations? They see the trains every day! You would think they understand where the money came from that provided their houses. We never should have agreed to the new expressway in the corridor."

Grady, Rick and Dan sat up and listened. It was a scene they had watched play out all their lives. Whenever expansion was in the works, the plant had to fight, tooth and nail, to get a plan approved and passed.

The three men in the conference room heard the others approaching so they stood up, heading to the coffee pot, pretending to be oblivious to the whole conversation taking place outside the door.

Mac called the meeting to a start and a hoard of bodies came into the large room from the outside waiting area, along with a handful of the Grady corporate executives. They all started pouring coffee and taking a seat. **"Janey!"** Mac called out. **"Get in here and get this screen up and running!"**

Grady looked Rick in the eye with a raise of his eyebrow, as he poured coffee into his friend's cup. "Not a happy camper today, is he?"

Rick looked back with a quiet glance and joked, "I can probably talk him into giving you your old job back, Bill. I'm sure it would come with a raise right about now."

"In a pig's eye, Buddy! I'm not ready to give up on that ranch job yet. I'm really not that fond of his outbursts when he gets like this. Our friendship's a lot better off, now that we're just best friends. I suffered through the yelling too many times in the past!" he said, as they chuckled and headed to their seats.

Mac watched the three as they sat at the big table. "Something you want to share with the group, Billy?"

He looked up at his old boss, "Now Mac, I know you aren't happy right now, but don't start in on me. I'm not the hired hand around here anymore. I was just telling Rick and Dan how much I love Janey's coffee." He grinned and held up his cup. "I do enjoy hangin' out with you all, though. It's good to smell the diesel coming from that yard again."

He looked on with a wry smile. "So, Bill, explain to me again just why everyone in town is calling you by my last name?" He knew the history of the name. All the CEOs on the ranch were called 'The Grady' since they were all hired away from the Grady Corporation, but he also knew this was the one comment his old friend wouldn't try to defend.

Grady just shook his head and looked down at his portfolio with a grimace. He gave Rick a slight elbow and whispered, *"Yep, he's having one of those days, alright."*

The meeting began and the overhead was turned on while Mac stood up and began to explain the problem. "The Harville Mining Company finally obtained final approval on the contract for the granite processing plant in Furline Canyon. We've been working on this plan for twenty years now. All of you in this room have probably had a hand in that at some point in your career. We have the agreements with the state and the Forest Service to do the road expansion from the back of the South Fork to Rails End. Everyone in this town wants to see it happen. It's only going to make it easier for them to drive up that road in the future to play and do their hunting."

He lifted his pointer and pointed to the old highway and followed it up to the South Fork, tracing it to the back. "Better road up the mountain, better road up the South Fork and the trucks will only haul the rock out from Monday to Thursday from Furline to Rails End. Everyone was happy with the plan. We even got the environmentalists on our side with all the improvements Harville and our company are throwing in to upgrade the fishing areas up the river. Everyone still gets to use the entire area from Friday to Sunday, without trucks being on the road. We even agreed to rebuild that dangerous bridge over the river where the North Fork Road starts to Red Mill Canyon, Bill. And doing that was a stretch for us to get this thing passed. But we agreed to it. You worked on that, so I don't need to say any more about it."

"Now here's the problem! To make this thing happen, we have to expand the rail lines through the Meadows Region going out of the valley toward the desert basin and the communities around Clearville. We gave the Meadowlands three plans on this. Last night, the board of supervisors for the county shot down the third plan. Too many complainers from the new housing tracts in the Meadows Region. We had the same problem when the airport expansion happened. That took two years to work out!"

He looked at Janey and she changed the maps on the overhead to a map of the rail lines. "All the new rails we planned in town are not a problem. My dad saw that one coming many years ago and purchased enough land in town. What the old man didn't see coming was just how many housing tracts would go in out in the Meadowlands. And I don't have to tell you how much of a pain in the butt that has been for all of us here in the corporate offices. We can't expand either of the lines on the North or the South side of the valley. The housing tracts complain about the noise as it is. We simply never expected the area to grow to the South. You all can thank the Givers Development Company for that one. There was no need to start putting houses in that part of the valley, but they did. It's been a sore spot for everyone since the day they broke ground out there. The Givers have always disregarded what was best for the entire region, if it meant a chance to line their pockets with money."

"Now the environmentalists are complaining about the *third* plan. And it's the same people who we gave so many concessions to for the road expansion up the mountain and in the South Fork. I need you all to put your thinking caps on and come up with a plan that'll make these guys happy. I'm not about to start tearing down mountains for a bypass. The cost is too prohibitive. The rest of the property out in the Meadowlands are private ranches and no one wants to sell. And I don't blame them. Cattle has been as much of a backbone in this community as the switching yards. To be honest, we all love the fact we can eat T-bone steaks for the price all of those city dwellers down in the southland pay for hamburger."

"Think it through, everyone. Come back and let me know what you come up with. We're up against a deadline. The offer on the mining agreement was only good for twenty years. The required signatures on the finalized agreement expire in three months if they're not signed. We don't want to have to start this whole process over again. Dealing with the federal bureaucrats is an expensive process and it's just not worth it to have to start from scratch again."

Valerie drove the expressway from Rails End to the Meadowlands with Crissy, to meet Jonathon for a quick lunch before she put her on the afternoon bus. She hated going behind Grady's back like this, but until she was up front with her father, she didn't want him knowing the girl was in town. As it stood, she wasn't happy with her for dragging the whole thing out for an extra day.

"Crissy, you be straight with your sisters about what's going on. The longer you hide this from them, the more obvious it will be. Hiding things just makes for hard feelings in the long run. You need their support!"

As the three sat and ate their lunch at the Whistle Stop Café, neither of them could enjoy the beauty of the garden and lawn as they sat on the deck in the corner of the outdoor, dining area. Jonathon was completely silent, and Crissy was full of emotions, so Valerie had to nudge the conversation along.

"You two need to tell me what your plan is for talking to your father." She looked with piercing eyes at Jonathon, making it clear to him it was time to quit fidgeting with that dusty cowboy hat and start talking. "What's your next step, Jonathon? You're the man of a family now, regardless of whether you're married or not."

After a long pause, she pulled her pocket Bible out of her purse and flipped through the pages to Ephesians chapter five:

"For you were once darkness, but now you are light in the Lord. Live as children of light. (for the fruit of the light consists in all goodness, righteousness and truth) and find out what pleases the Lord. Have nothing to do with the fruitless deeds of darkness, but rather expose them. It is shameful even to mention what the disobedient do in secret. But everyone exposed by the light becomes visible and everything that is illuminated becomes a light. That is why it is said: "Wake up, sleeper, rise from the dead, and Christ will shine on you."

-Ephesians 5:8-14

She reached over to Jonathon's hat and took it from his hand, putting it on the table. She then took his hand in hers and held it. "Jonathon, building a family starts with knowing God. Have you ever accepted Christ into your life?"

He looked up slowly and searched for a reply. "I've gone to church before. I ... I wasn't raised in a church family."

She smiled. "Jonathon, the Bible clearly tells us everyone is born into sin. When Adam and Eve sinned, it cast every man and woman on this earth into being born sinful. We all come from the first family on earth. We don't know anything different. Christ came to bridge that gap between man and God. When he died on the cross, he took our place in punishment. Our guilt was put on his shoulders if we accept him and admit we're sinners. It's a free gift, and Christ said he's the only door to God the Father. All must go through that door to be a child of God. Each man is free to accept or reject it. If you accept it, you will have life in heaven for eternity. But if you reject the plan the Creator of this earth provides, a plan He created long before the earth was formed, then you'll go to hell."

She let that sink in for a minute and added, "Life on earth is the first step. It's the training ground for what God has planned for all of us in eternity after we leave this earth. The question is, are you willing to give up your own will and give it over to Christ and live the life he wants you to live. I don't think there's any missing the fact the two of you have messed up. But there's forgiveness in Christ and right here, right now is where the tire meets the pavement, Jonathon. If you want success, true success in life, it starts by admitting you're a sinner and need God to help you sort out this mess and turn it into a strong family. A loving family!"

He simply listened. It was all new to him.

"I want you to come to church with me this Sunday up at the ranch. The more you attend, the more you will begin to understand God. I'll sit with you if you want me to. As for telling Grady what's going on ... well ... you'll have to cross that bridge when Crissy's ready to talk with her father."

She turned the page in her Bible. "I want to read another verse from this same chapter in Ephesians to both of you."

Wives, submit yourselves to your own husbands as you do to the Lord. For the husband is the head of the wife as Christ is the head of the church, his body, of which he is the Savior. Now as the church submits to Christ, so also wives should submit to their husbands in everything.

Husbands, love your wives, just as Christ loved the church and gave himself up for her to make her holy, cleansing her by the washing with water through the word, and to present her to himself as a radiant church, without stain or wrinkle or any other blemish, but holy and blameless. In this same way, husbands ought to love their wives as their own bodies. He who loves his wife loves himself.

-Ephesians 5:22-28

"It's a big responsibility, Jonathon, but it's a responsibility God helps you with. You're the man. You're the one who has to lead both of you through this situation. The two of you have to make some big decisions. I suggest you spend a lot of time on the phone talking in the next few weeks."

She pulled a new cell phone from her purse, giving it to Crissy, along with the charger. "I bought this for you, Crissy. I'm expecting a call from you every week to let me know what's going on. Don't drag your feet on this. You have to tell your dad soon. Call me when you need to talk." She reached across the table and took Crissy's hand. "You're not alone in this, Crissy. I'm here to help you!"

"Jonathon, I have something for you also." She reached into her purse again and withdrew a new Bible. "I've marked the chapter I just read from. It's a great place to start reading to understand the man God expects you to be, and the husband and father who you need to become for Crissy and the baby. I've also marked a set of pages in the book of Romans. There's a series of Scriptures I highlighted on those pages. Just start at the first chapter and go to each page I marked, one at a time, and read them. It's called the Romans Road. These Scriptures really helped me when I first began to understand God and what Christ was offering to each of us." She took his hand again. "These are really great Scriptures, Jonathon. I want you to promise me you'll read these before Sunday morning."

As she stared at the young man with an intent look, he said, "Uhm ... I mean, yeah! I'll read them, Doctor Dobbins."

"You're not alone. All you have to do is talk to God and He will answer you. Just take time each day to talk to Him. You'll see!"

She paid for the bill and the three of them walked to the bus stop outside, giving Crissy a big hug as they put her on the bus. As the two watched the bus pull away, Valerie turned to him and gave him a hug. "Look, you may want to just run from all this right now. I know exactly how you're feeling, Jonathon. I had something really bad happen to me when I was a young girl. All I wanted to do was run from it. I will always be thankful for a friend who helped me through it and taught me about Christ and His love. Don't run from it. Run to God and let Him sort it all out for you! That book, Romans, also says all things work for good for those who trust in Him."

She knew she had said enough. She got in her car and headed back to Rails End.

- 6 -

CITY SLICKERS

The following Saturday, Grady sat up in his bed as he heard gun blasts, a series of rifle shots which exploded from near the pavilion at the end of the meadow! He grabbed his jeans from the bed post and pulled them on. He could hear screaming, a woman's voice. He was jerking his boots on as he tried to stand, stumbling around the room in the dark and hitting the wall. The screams were getting louder, a horrible cry for help! He became frantic. It was Valerie's voice he was hearing!

He ran to the fireplace and jerked his 30/30 from the gun rack on the wall. He accidently busted through the door, breaking the screen in two and cutting his forehead on the jagged, broken wood as the locked latch held tightly to the doorframe. He leapt from the porch, wearing only his jeans and boots, as he ran full stride with the rifle stock in his hand. He could see a few other men running in the direction of Jed's cabin as their wives stood on the porch with a robe or blanket wrapped around them in the gradient light of the early dawn.

He cut between two cabins and hit the meadow, hopping over rocks and bushes, his eyes scanning in all directions. Donavan was approaching the cabin in the Polaris with a halt of the vehicle that left a dust cloud in the air. He watched him jump from the seat as the lanky cowboy leapt onto the porch before the other men arrived.

He approached the cabin and could see Jed in a tussle with two men who were holding hunting rifles as the screams were coming from the cabin. Jed was shoving them back as he yelled at them. He gave Donavan a wide berth to control what was taking place in the cabin as he ran straight for the fight taking place in Jed's back yard. He tossed the short field rifle to his other hand, catching his fingers through the hand lever and flipping the stock of the western rifle forward. He jerked it back to load a round in the chamber. He stopped fifteen feet short of the group with the barrel of the rifle trained on the men in orange, hunting jackets, as Jed struggled to get up off the ground. He walked in a circle around the two, holding the rifle at his shoulder as he pointed it at them, ordering the two to drop their weapons.

Jason Twibley ran up to Jed as Mike Pratt backed his boss up, pointing another rifle at them, standing in nothing but the bottoms of his white, long johns and hiking boots. "What's going on, Grady?"

"Put the guns down, now!" he yelled at the men as blood ran down his face. They laid the hunting rifles on the ground and put their hands in the air. As he focused his eyes, he realized one of the men was only a teenage kid.

They listened to Valerie crying in the house while Jed brushed the dirt from his pants and handed Grady his hanky, picking up his cowboy hat. "These two dimwits were standing right behind my cabin firing their weapons. Scared the '*you know what*' out of all of us."

Jason walked over to the men and picked up their rifles, walking to the Polaris and unloading them, one at a time, tossing them on the seat.

"Did they shoot into the house?" he asked, trying to make sense of what had happened.

"No … uhm … I don't think so. I don't really know yet! I ran out the back door to find these two knuckle heads firing their guns toward the tree line."

"Start talkin'!" Grady demanded as he looked at the older man and lowered his gun, wiping his bleeding face with the cloth.

"We were just shooting at a buck we saw in the trees. That's all! We weren't even pointing our guns at the house. I don't know why she was screaming."

"Mike, Jason, take these two idiots to the office while I go see what's going on inside. Find out who they are. For now, they're under arrest until I get this whole thing sorted out." He turned and quickly walked to the back door, throwing the screen open with a bang against the pantry closet as he entered Betsy's kitchen. He walked to the dining room, unloading his gun and laying it across the center of the dining room table, heading for the hallway.

Donavan stood in the hall waving his hands, warning him to simmer down. "She's alright, Grady. She wasn't shot, but she's very *freaked out* right now. Betsy's with her and I don't really understand what's going on. I checked her out. She's not hurt."

As he brushed past the tall, ranch mechanic, Donavon pulled on his arm and said, "Calm down, Grady! You need to be gentle with her right now!" looking him in the eye.

"Then why was she screaming like that?"

"I told you. I don't understand what's going on. Just catch your breath and wait a minute. Betsy has her calmed down. She's talking to her."

He paced the hall for thirty seconds, agitated, and turned and shoved the door open, walking into the room. Valerie was sitting in a fetal position in the corner of the room, sobbing, with a pillow up to her face. Betsy stood and faced him, forcing him back a few feet and ordered, "Grady, just wait! Hear me out first. Donny! Please come in here! I need you to sit with her for a minute while I talk to Grady!"

Donavan entered the room as she gently forced Grady out. "Meet me on the porch. Just do what I tell you!" Donavan walked to the sobbing woman and knelt on his knees next to her, rubbing her arm gently to comfort her.

She marched him to the porch and sat him down on the wicker couch, taking a seat next to him. Jed ascended the three steps and pulled a rocker over to join them.

"What's going on, Betsy?" he said in an angry tone.

Jed leaned forward toward him, grabbing his arm. "Now, Grady, just stop talking and listen. There's some things you need to know about Valerie. We didn't think it was our place to be discussing this with you. It was her thing to be telling you. Now it's time to talk about it, so just listen!" Jed removed his coat and handed it to him, as he sat without a shirt in the freezing, morning air.

She took his hand and gently held it. "Valerie and I were out to lunch about a year ago, just about the time you two got really serious about dating. She needed to talk about her past and what happened to her as a child. Do you remember our conversation that night in the guest room ... the first night she stayed on the ranch? I told you she wasn't the strong person you perceived her to be."

He nodded. "I remember the whole conversation."

"Valerie had a brother. I know you don't know that yet. She doesn't talk about him. When she was ten years old, she and her brother were home alone and a man broke into their house." She began to struggle a little as tears filled her eyes. "The man shot her brother, Grady. He killed him. Valerie was standing right there in the room with them. She watched the whole thing happen. It's haunted her all of her life. The boy was dead before they even reached the hospital."

The confused man looked down for a minute as the two sat in silence, looking at him. She said, "She was screaming in there because she was asleep when those two in the backyard started shooting their rifles. It terrified her. They were standing right next to the window of the guest room when they fired their guns. She thought she was back in her parent's house with that man standing there, shooting her brother."

"I've taken her shooting. We've done it plenty of times. She's never once complained about my rifle or mentioned any of this."

She narrowed her eyes as she looked at him. "Do you know what a girl wants most from a man? She wants to feel protected and safe. Every woman fears being a victim when she's alone. Have you ever met a woman who doesn't lock the door when her husband's gone? When she's with you, she feels safe. The fact you have that old field rifle with you everywhere you go is a comfort to her. What did I tell you that night when we sat on the bed?"

He looked up and suddenly made sense of the entire conversation. "You told me to do right by her and protect her."

"Exactly! And you're about to marry a woman who takes the meaning of that even more seriously than most women. The average woman just has fears about it. She lived through it. She watched a loved one die."

Jed stood up and walked into the house, pouring a cup of coffee for both of them. He came back to the porch and handed Grady a cup. "Have a sip and just relax for a while, Cowboy. Let Betsy spend some time with her till she's ready to talk to you. It's time for her to talk this all out and when it's over, she's probably gonna be very embarrassed. The whole ranch heard her screaming. After what happened last year, I can tell you one of the things she fears the most is having her weaknesses on display in front of everyone. I guess that just makes her a normal person."

Betsy stood up and walked into the house, leaving the two men to sit on the porch in silence for a while. She went back to the room, thanking Donavan and asking him to go out on the porch. Valerie stared up at her with a look of embarrassment. Betsy sat down with her on the floor, her back to the wall, and placed their hands together.

She leaned into Betsy's shoulder and slid her arm into the woman's, and they sat for a minute in silence. "I'm sorry, Betsy. I didn't mean to scare you like that. I still don't understand what was going on. All I could think of was the past when I heard those guns going off."

"We have rules up here. They weren't supposed to be firing the guns in the village. Red Mill Canyon is a hunting preserve. That was the original intent of the whole Association when they bought this old canyon. It's not often we see the families here in the last few years. Now that the ranch is being sold, we have ten families in the cabins right now. They know it's their last chance to use the place and do hunting. And before the summer is over, it's only gonna get worse."

Betsy quietly held her for a few minutes. "You need to go out and talk with him. It's time to discuss the past. The entire ranch heard you screaming." She chuckled, "All the hired hands were up here half-dressed and one of 'em was standing in his underwear. But in times like this, it's good to know the men on this ranch take quick action when they think someone's in trouble."

She struggled to a standing position and reached out her hand, helping Valerie up. She took the comforter from the bed, wrapping it around her. "Give me a minute to shoo Jed and Donny off the porch and then come out and talk to Grady. He was a bit confused about what was happening. I told him about your brother, Valerie. But you need to explain the whole story to him. He's the man you're about to marry. It's time for him to know. I'll get breakfast cooking while you talk to him."

Grady crossed his arms, staring at Jed and Donavan. "Why don't you go to the office and have a talk with those two idiots? You need to go over the rules with them about hunting up here. Donny, wake all the staff up and tell them to put the word out to anyone who's staying on the ranch right now. We're having a meeting at ten o'clock to make sure they all know where they can and can't hunt. Tell Owen that no one parks a car beyond the security gate without a copy of the rules in their hand. I want the head of each family to come into the office, from this point on, to sign off that they understand the rules before they even stop at the cabin they reserved. No one gets a key to their cabin without signing off on the rules! We have about a dozen of 'em on the ranch right now. In a few weeks this place is going to be packed."

The two men headed out and Grady took the coffee cups in, returning to the porch. Valerie walked out in her pajamas with the quilted comforter wrapped around her. He looked up at her frail form and her face quivered with tears. "I'm sorry. I should have spoken with you about this long before now." She sat on the couch, turning her body to lay on the long, soft cushion as she rested across his lap. He wrapped his arms around her body and held her tightly as she laid her head on his chest. Just like that morning after the storm as he had laid on the bed in his cabin holding her weak body, Betsy could hear her start sobbing as Grady pulled the comforter tighter up around her.

Betsy was right! She wasn't the strong-natured person who she pretended to be. Valerie had weaknesses she hid from the world. Now her secret was out. It caused him to love her even more, as he held her in his arms while she cried. "I love you, girl. And I'm here for you. Don't be afraid, Val."

He pulled the hanky from his pocket she had given him the previous autumn, wiping the tears from her face. "The night you gave me this hanky, I cleared my conscience and told you my big secret. Now I know yours. It's all out, Val. No more secrets between us." He looked into her eyes and said, "Pursue me, Valerie! Pursue me for the rest of our life!"

She smiled as she heard him repeat the very words she had said to him so many months before, the words which had wiped away all of the anger and hurt, sealing their future. She clung tight to his chest and started crying again.

- 7 -

THE MEETING

Jed drove his truck down Mainstreet on a warm July morning as he and Grady were making business stops in Rails End. He said, "Jonathon was over to the house last night. You're not gonna believe this. We spent a lot of time in the Word together. I led the boy to the Lord."

"Jonathon ... Jonathon Harris?" Grady had a look of surprise.

"The boy's been real broken up about something lately. He's been stayin' away from all the others in the bunk house. It was a bit of a surprise to me also."

As the two talked, the steam whistle at the switching yards spewed a loud scream which echoed across the small town, announcing the noon shift-change. He looked at his watch, "Man, where has the day gone? I can't believe it's lunch time already."

"Why don't we head down to the Cougar Lounge," Jed suggested with a twinkle in his eye. "Today's Wednesday. Pastrami sandwiches, Cowboy! They make the best ones in the entire Meadows area. They grill them up right with sauerkraut and dill pickles in the middle."

He glanced at him and smiled as he looked out the right-side window. *"This man loves his sandwiches!"* he mused as he watched the crew of men jumping from the engines which were being parked on the tracks across the switching yards. "I don't care where we eat. I'm for the Cougar. It's been months since I was in the place."

Jed pulled his four-wheel drive into the gravel parking lot to the sound of crushed pebbles, stopping near the door. They grabbed their hats, heading inside.

Grady searched across the darkness of the large bar which was the favorite meeting place for a lot of the men who worked the train yards. He pointed to a door at the back. "Let's sit in the back room. This place is gonna be busier than the cow pens on branding day pretty soon."

He smiled at the waitress, "Give us a booth in the back. I don't like all the noise." Misty Connor led the cowboys into the dark room. "How about the booth next to the planter? And give us a couple of those pastrami sandwiches and some teas."

She dusted the seats and the table off with a rag. "Sorry, Bill. Not too many people want to use these seats lately. Mostly, the room just gets used for meetings these days when people want to be left alone."

"That suits me just fine, Misty. After the last eighteen months up in the canyon, I'm not used to being around crowds. I like the peace and quiet." They each slid into a side of the booth.

"What have you got on the purchase of the ranch, Grady? We're gonna need to get our offer in soon. It's gonna take a while to get all the details done if we buy it."

"Well, from what I hear, there aren't too many offers for the Canyon. Just a couple. Old Drake down at the hardware store put in an offer. He bids on anything that goes up for sale that isn't a house. I suppose he's probably looking toward retirement and just wants a place to be left alone where there's peace and quiet. I know he plans on dismantling the cabins or selling them whole. Not a bad idea. Pay a little back on the purchase price of the property."

"So, tell me. What do *you* see for those cabins in the future? It's an awful lot of work, maintaining that town. Those eighty cabins keep Donny and I pretty busy in the wintertime. Not so bad as it used to be. None of the families really use them much anymore. If you ask me, they're a fire hazard."

He looked up with one eye open, "Those old cabins are worth a lot more standing than they are torn down. We can rent them out to people who come up for the horseback riding, fishing and hunting.

We can even turn some of them into small stores if we get enough interest from the tourists who traipse up and down the South Fork Canyon. It's only five miles below the ranch and cars are passing the front gate all day to head up to the sequoias."

Misty brought their pastrami sandwiches and drinks in, setting them on the table. Jed's eyes just about bugged out as he looked at the red meat, piled high between the Jewish rye, with pickles and sauerkraut falling out of the middle around each plate. "Is there anything else? It's getting pretty busy in there."

"No, Misty. I think we just want to be left alone to talk business for a while." He handed the waitress two twenties. "I think that should more than cover it. Keep the rest."

"You're a good man, Bill! Thanks for the tip! And don't be such a stranger. It's been a while." She put the pitcher of tea on the table and hurried out of the room.

As the two men dug into the sandwiches, he said, "I don't know who the other bidder is. Doug Thomas told me they don't want to be revealed. From what I understand, they're pretty serious buyers. These days, serious buyers mean developers."

The two men heard the door open with a chorus of noises and voices, and silence engulfed the room as it shut again. He looked through the plastic, green plants at a familiar face and furrowed his brow, looking back at Jed with a quiet voice. *"It's Jared Brine. Best we just stop talking about this for now. I don't want the guy to know we're even in the room. The last thing I need is him and his family getting all mad again about their dad's arrest last year. A few of them got pretty mouthy with me during the trial."*

Jared took a seat at the long row of tables on the other side of the planter, completely unaware anyone was in the dark room. He pulled a cigarette from his pocket and lit it, putting his beer down with a loud clunk as he sat at the table. He lifted a phone from his pocket, dialing, as they watched. "I'm here. The room's empty. Bring them here and we can talk."

He no sooner ended his call and the phone rang. "Yeah!" he said with an annoyed tone. "Oh ... sorry, Aunt Peggy. No ... no ... it's all taken care of, don't worry. The money's already collected and in the account. Ron and Uncle Jack are on their way over here right now with the others."

As Grady and Jed listened, trying to piece some things together in their heads, Jared got nasty as he talked on the phone. "Look, you don't worry about them folk up in Red Mill! If they lose the bid, they're gone! If they win the bid ... well ... we have a plan to take care of that and make sure they don't come up with the money. This isn't about getting back at them, Peggy. It's a business deal, but don't you worry. If they do come in with a higher price, I'm sure you'll be satisfied after we're done with them."

He shut the phone off and the two cowboys stared at each other. Grady turned his head to the side and just stared at Jed, holding his finger up to warn him to be silent. One-by-one, over the next ten minutes, people came through the door. First was Ron Givers from the Owners Association. The next to come through the door were a couple of Jared's family members. The last to enter was Darcy Jenkins' father, Jack Jenkins. The group settled in on the other side of the planter and the meeting started.

Jack's voice became louder than the others to make it clear it was time to talk. "Ron and I spent five years putting this plan together. That bunch up at Red Mill has made it a little harder for us, but the plan goes forward now that the Association wants to sell. I never wanted to see any of our relatives in jail. But in the end, that Bill Simmons and his bunch simply made the whole process easier for getting the Association to sell. Now we just have to have the higher price."

Jared crossed his arms, sitting back in the chair. "Peggy wants revenge, Uncle Jack. It's the only thing she has to look forward to now days. She'll be in that place for five years."

He became angry. "Peggy knew what she was getting into the day we moved her here and bought into the Owners Association! She'll retire rich when she gets out! The houses we're going to build in that canyon will fetch the highest prices in the Sierras. Peggy needs to understand this is about the money, not getting even. You just make sure if we get outbid it's taken care of. Do you understand?" He stared at Ron with a humbler look. "Sorry Ron, I don't mean to be so angry about your stepmom. What have the lawyers said about the transfer of ownership of Five Star?"

"There's no way out of this! The woman who bought the company has called in all our debt. She's called in all debts of any accounts in Rails End. She filed a lien against our land development company. That was one third of all our cash reserves, so we're going into this bid on Red Mill way under-capitalized for the kind of bid we need to be making. To make matters worse, we lost about a hundred thousand in cash flow when the cops raided Peggy, Joe and Darcy's houses."

Jack said, "I thought you said all debt for the development company was deferred for thirty years when you sold the company to him?"

"It was, according to the contract of sale. The only thing that could negate the agreement is someone else purchasing the company from him. When a corporation is sold, all agreements are off and have to be renegotiated. And this is what really upsets me. Mr. Drake from the hardware store. I had him on the books for a thirty-thousand-dollar loan when I sold Five Star. This new woman who now owns it, she wrote his entire debt off for some reason. Drake's one of the people we're going up against in the bidding process. It not only makes us weaker, but it makes him stronger."

"You screwed up with the sale, Ron. Just admit it. The man was just purchasing Five Star to strip it and sell it."

"Jack, I piled so much of our debt onto the deal that no one would want to purchase the company from him. He was an idiot. He had no clue what he was doing. He had no plan to sell the company. He told me she forced a deal on him to make him sell Five Star to her. She overpaid for the amount of the negative balance on the books. Then she foreclosed on all debt as the new owner. He didn't strip the company. She did and paid more than the debt was worth to do it? It makes no sense."

Ron said, "Jared, we all lost family members to that

investigation. I will deal with my mom. You just take care of your end of it. If she calls you again, you tell her to call me and start talking with me. I don't want to lose this opportunity. It's taken too many years to put it together."

Jed looked up at Grady and turned his head slightly, giving him a silent warning and a look of caution. He could see the anger building up in him as his mind was putting the pieces together at a rapid pace. *"They're all related! How did they keep this quiet? Just like the Givers had done with the Red Mill Canyon over forty years earlier, they were bilking the Association and trying to steal the property again."*

The men finished and started clearing out of the room. Grady waited till the door finally shut behind them. "This is like a bad dream that won't go away!" The tall cowboy let out a cuss word. "How did they keep the fact they were all related a secret?"

"Don't talk like that. You know how I feel about cussin'. We need to start takin' this issue to prayer, not getting mouthy about it."

He looked down, "Sorry Jed. I just can't believe this! I thought we were rid of that bunch when the trial was over. It's obvious we don't have a clue what's going on. No one does."

"Well, we know one thing for sure now. Jack Jenkins and Ron Givers are the ring leaders, not Darcy! I'm kinda' surprised Sheriff Jackson missed that one in his investigation last year."

"You can only run an investigation on what you know about. But one thing's for sure. He's gonna know now! But we're gonna wait a few days before we say anything to the others. We just need to pray about this. I don't want to draw everyone else into it. I think you, Donny, Betsy and I need to have a meeting tonight. Can we do dinner at your house?"

"I'll call the old girl right now. And I'll have her fetch Donny and let him know we need to talk." Grady handed him the cell phone.

Jed and Grady pulled onto Mainstreet to the sound of two ambulances streaking down the road past them with lights and sirens going. He texted Valerie. *"Jed and I are in town. Getting ready to head up the mountain."* A few minutes later his phone announced, *"Val Gal."* Jed looked at him with a laugh. "What happened to Valerie Dobbins?"

He smiled back, "I changed it yesterday while she was takin' a nap. I fixed hers also."

Grady pressed the button and waited. *"Sooo, Cowboy!* I see you messed with my phone. From now on I sleep with it in my pocket!" she said with a laugh.

"Just trying to keep things in the proper perspective, Val Gal," he said with a grin on his face.

"Come by the clinic. I need to see you for a few minutes."

He looked at Jed, "Okay if we make a pit stop at the clinic for a while?"

"No skin off my back. I haven't seen Valerie since summer started, with all the work we've been doing on the ranch the last few months. All those owners visiting the ranch have been keeping us busy."

They walked into the clinic to find the staff on high alert. Two ambulances were pulling into the back of the clinic and the staff was darting everywhere while Dr. Mansfield was giving orders. The two men followed the group down the hall to the emergency receiving area and Grady stopped short of the end of the hallway. Jed hesitated, looking back at him. "You alright? You look kinda' white in the face."

He looked at him with a grimace. "Bad memories, my friend. The last time I saw two ambulances being unloaded in this area, one had Missy in it and the other was Celia's dead body. To be honest, I couldn't tell which was which." His eyes began to well up with tears and he turned away, walking back to the lobby.

After a few minutes, he could hear Valerie and Jed walking up the hall. "That was a bad night, Jed. It was a long night for all of us! I don't blame him for not wanting to be in there right now!"

She came into the room and sat next to Grady, who was sitting with his elbows on his knees, running his large hands through his hair. "Hey, you ok, Bill?" She put her arm around her fiancé with one hand, and held his hand with the other.

He ran a hand over his eyes, wiping them. "I'm alright, really I am. I just got a flash back of the night of the accident when I saw those vehicles being unloaded. It's been a year and a half since I was even in the emergency room."

Jed looked down at the floor as she rubbed his back with her hand. "It was a bad night for all of us. Actually, you weren't alone. This is the first time since the accident we've had two ambulances at once like that. I was thinking about the same thing."

He asked, "What's up? We saw them coming from the switching yards with their lights and sirens on."

"They had another accident in the engine house. They were removing some parts from one of the locomotives and a cable broke. Dr. Mansfield is going to need me in there. I only have a minute. Bill, I needed to tell you that Crissy's coming in a few weeks. She called me today."

He looked up at her with questioning eyes. "Why didn't she call me?"

She looked at him hesitantly. "Crissy … well … we've been talking on the phone a lot lately. She's going through some things she needed advice about." Jed walked away from the conversation and stood in the hall, leaning against the wall and watching the saga taking place at the other end. After a few seconds of silence, she said, "Women's things. Celia's not here for her to talk to anymore, so she called me. She wants to come home and see you. She's decided she needed to be at the ranch for the rest of the summer. All three of the girls are coming, Shawny and Missy also."

He picked up his hat and put it on. "Well, I guess it's a good thing if Crissy's talking to you when she needs advice. That's a good sign."

She wasn't quite sure how to answer that, so she smiled and pursed her lips tight as she nodded. She ran her fingers over the scar on his forehead and made a pouting look of empathy. "I have to go, Cowboy," giving him a quick kiss as they stood. "I'll see you on Saturday. The girls will be here the day after the winning bid on the ranch is announced."

"Val, you need to keep the this bid meeting in prayer. They open the bids for the ranch in three weeks." Grady stopped short and hesitated as he thought about the meeting they overheard at lunch. Jed knew exactly why he was hesitating. He stood behind Valerie, nodding his head toward the door with a furrowed brow, to signal to Grady he needed to end it right there and be silent.

The two men climbed into the cab of the truck and Jed waited to turn the engine over. "You need to keep Valerie out of what's going on for a few days, boss. She's got enough to deal with at the moment." As Jed drove out of the parking lot, he knew he had no clue what he meant when he said it. Betsy and Jed kept no secrets from each other. Betsy had already put the pieces of the puzzle together just watching what had taken place over the last few months. The Gentrys had taken the issue to prayer every night since she did.

As he pulled onto the street all he could think of was, "God help us all when Grady finds out. And God help Johnny Harris when it happens!" He had spent several nights sitting on his porch with the boy going over Scriptures and praying with him. Jonathon hadn't breached the subject with him yet, and he was just fine with that until Crissy stepped off the bus.

BRIAN VOIGT

- 8 -

LA SONRISA

Valerie paddled hard in the water, screaming out a pleading laugh as Grady chased her. He grabbed her, pushing her down hard underwater. "I'm not so old *now* am I, girl!" he said as she came up for air. She grabbed his neck, wrapping both arms around it so he couldn't push her under again. Jed and Betsy watched from the ledge with a chuckle, eating their lunch at one of the café tables.

She checkmated his maneuver wrapping her legs around his waist, making him tread water to hold both of them up. She did the only thing she could think of to stop him from winning the tussle. She pressed their faces together and started kissing him. And after a short ten seconds, he gave in and quit fighting. He returned the kiss, only this time it was on the mouth.

Jed tried to look off and give them their privacy, pretending not to notice what was taking place below at the other end of the water pool. He admired the beauty of the blooming trees and the large walls of rock, which ascended up high above him.

Betsy joked, "I'm startin' to think waiting all summer for this wedding might have been a mistake," watching the two swimmers who were locked in a passionate embrace. "If this goes on much longer, the poor boy's gonna drown trying to hold up the two of them like that."

One minute of affection turned into two as Valerie clung onto him and they shared the moment, oblivious to the audience up on the ledge.

Jed clapped his hands and called out, **"Okay, you two**

teenagers! Let's not forget this is a chaperoned date here!" Jed looked at Betsy, who was staring at him with a look of displeasure. "Well, Betsy dear, I'm not about to yell 'get a hotel room.' They just might take me seriously," he laughed.

"Let 'em have their moment, Jed. They're happy right now. Lord knows things are gonna get pretty dicey in a few weeks. I haven't seen 'em having fun like this for a long time."

After a few minutes of kissing, Grady nodded up toward the ledge. "I think the old folks are getting restless. It's time to get dried off."

She looked up at the beauty of the blooming trees as she held onto him. "Maybe we could just sneak up here and spend our honeymoon week surrounded by all this beauty, Grady."

He laughed as he pushed her away. "Now I *know* it's time to get out of the pool!"

She pulled him back with a serious look. "I'm looking forward to our honeymoon, Bill Simmons. I've been waiting for a long time." She kissed him one more time.

He looked her in the eyes, "Don't you know it, Val. Two more months. Two more months and you get to wear that pretty, white dress." As he turned to swim to the edge, she pushed down on his shoulders and dunked him one more time, swimming quickly to the edge of the pool in retreat, with a laugh and a scream which echoed off the rocks as he tried to grab her wet foot.

Grady asked the group assembled at the dinner table in the Gentry's dining room to stand, and they all took hands to pray before the meal. "I want you all to know the facts of the bid meeting that's about to take place in a few weeks. We're up against two other bidders. During the meal we need to spend some time talking this out. When we're done, I plan to take the issue to prayer." The group bowed their heads as Jed prayed over the meal. *"Lord, thank you for the food we're about to eat. This is gonna be a long month, Lord. I ask for strength and patience on all of us here, Father. And whatever the outcome of this month, guide us. Make your love known to us, Lord."*

Betsy and Valerie put the platter of barbequed spareribs on the table that the boys had smoked while the others were up at Sonrisa. They served the dishes full of corn bread stuffing, corn on the cob, fresh baked rolls and salad as everyone filled their plates full.

"Good job on the ribs, you two!" Grady said to Jonathon and Jason, as Jed looked on with a certain amount pride. "You boys have learned a lot about that smoker." He smiled with a wink at Jed.

As they ate, he outlined the bidding process for everyone. "We're up against two sets of bidders. The group I'm concerned about is something Jed, Donny, Betsy and I have been spending a lot of time in prayer about. There's some things you all need to know about that. Jed and I found out the secret bidder is the Givers."

Valerie looked up with concern. "How can the Givers be a bidder? They're one of the owners. Didn't you say they owned a huge portion of the Association?"

"Well, Val, that's where the rub comes in." He drew in a deep breath. "It's time to put your big boy panties on, folks. The next part is gonna be hard to swallow. The Givers are related to Darcy, Joe *and* Peggy. They're all one big family."

Everyone stopped eating and stared at him for several seconds as the group tried to absorb the bad news. "You have got to be kidding! This is like a horrible dream!"

Jonathon said, "Please tell me you're joking! You ran that bunch off. I thought they were in prison now!"

"They *are* in prison. As it turns out, Peggy's Ron Givers stepmother. And there's even worse news. Jack Jenkins, who's Darcy's father, is the ringleader behind the entire bunch of cockroaches. Jed and I happened to be in the room with them and overheard their meeting about the upcoming bids. We were having lunch at the Cougar in that dark room in the back, and they didn't know we were there. We overheard the whole thing. It turns out they've all been in on what was taking place at the ranch over the last five years. As near as I've been able to piece together, the Givers started moving their relatives into the valley and keeping it a secret they're all related. Peggy's Jack Jenkins and Joe Brine's sister-in-law. Ron Givers is her stepson. They were bilking the ranch to pay for some kind of plan to get the owners to sell in the future. They plan to level the property and subdivide it for expensive estate houses."

Donavan said, "When did old man Givers get remarried?"

"When Shawna Givers passed away, Ron took over the family business and his father left Rails End. Apparently, he remarried."

Valerie shook her head. "Tell me you've talked with Jimmy Jackson about this? What's the Sheriff's department doing about the whole thing?"

He cleared his throat, "I have a meeting on Monday with Jimmy. But for the moment, there isn't much he *can* do about it. He's already arrested and tried the three who were causing all the problems. They're in jail. He needs proof to drag anyone else into it. The fact that Jed and I are bidders could leave us out of any future testimony. It's a conflict of interest. It would only strengthen their case if we testified about what we heard in that room if another criminal case went to trial."

Jonathon asked, "How did Sheriff Jackson miss the fact they were all related during the investigation?"

"Well, there isn't any law against being related. And if you don't tell anyone you're related, then no one knows to ask about it. No one had a clue about this!"

Jed said, "It gets worse than that. We overheard them talking about doing something bad if we win the bid, something to try and stop us from being able to go through with it. We don't know what, but I can tell you we all need to keep our eyes and ears open. They're gonna do something. We just don't know what. Now legally, the Givers can't buy the property without incurring a lot of liability and lawsuits. Half of the owners are selling to try to stop the other half who are filing the lawsuits. But that doesn't stop the Brines or the Jenkins from gaining ownership. They can set this thing up however they want using their relatives as a shadow company. But in the end, the Givers will be a part of the whole thing. They own the construction company."

Grady looked downcast in front of the whole group. "My family went through this same kind of thing with the Givers, back before the Canyon was sold to the Association. They succeeded in cutting my family out of our ownership of the area. But they made one mistake. They should have never hired me to come back up here. I've never been out for revenge over what happened to my Granddaddy. But now I'm here and I don't intend to leave. I'm playing this out to the end. If that means fixing what they did to him, then so be it."

Jed looked up with concern. "I completely understand if any of you want out of this deal. Betsy and I have already talked it out. We spent the best days of our life up here. We even raised our kids on this ranch. This is where we intend to grow old. That church out there is alive again and that's been a prayer of ours for years."

As the group discussed the issue, Valerie, Jonathon and Jason were angry and had reservations about going forward. Donavan stood in the middle of the argument and banged his coffee cup down hard on the table. "I don't have any real family other than my mother! Everyone sitting at this table is my family! I'm getting too old to go back to the rail yards. I think you all need to be thankful we have a couple of men who have the wisdom these two have. I'm in it to the end and that's all I got to say about it!" He simply walked out with a bang of the screen door.

After everyone left the cabin, Jed and Grady sat at the table in total silence. Jed looked up at him with a chuckle. "You have to give him credit. Donny may be a quiet man, and he don't have a lot of eloquence, but when he speaks his mind, he sure can clear a room."

Grady and Jed sat on the porch of the cabin house and sipped their coffee as they rocked in the rockers, watching the scene that was playing out across the road in the pavilion. Valerie had gathered the other three men, including Donavan, and they were talking out their feelings about going forward. They all would be an owner if they succeeded in winning the bid, and for Jonathon and Jason, it would be an opportunity which rarely comes for young men of their limited experience. Grady's money was backing the bid, but they would all buy into the ownership with hard work as the plan developed into something bigger and more profitable.

Jed looked at him with a quiet smile as they watched. "Ya' know, boss, this entire operation is a family up here. We eat together, work together and all of us have had a hand in the success of it in the last year. I realize you and Valerie took the brunt of what happened last year." He muttered quietly, "Still makes me angry when I think about what happened in that board meeting last November."

"I appreciate you saying that. It hurt Valerie pretty badly with what happened that night. She told me afterwards she was gonna break up with me before that big storm hit. Ya' know, God has a way of making bad things change for the good. I've never been one to buy into all that success-faith doctrine nonsense. I look back on my life and the meaningful memories come from the hard times God put on my family. They were growing experiences. That big storm was so devastating, and Val almost died in that old barn on the South Fork. But in the end, it pushed us closer together." He looked Jed in the eye. "Pushed you and me closer together! And the only way I have to thank you for what you and Donny did that night is to make this thing happen for us all, regardless of what it takes."

Jed stood from his rocker. "I want to show you a few Scriptures I've been lookin' at as we've been praying about this whole thing." He went in the house and brought their family Bible out and sat back in his rocker. He handed him the leather-bound Bible Valerie gave him. "Open your Bible to Romans chapter eight and start reading verses 14-17."

Grady found the Scripture:

"For those who are led by the Spirit of God are the children of God. The Spirit you received brought about your adoption to sonship. And by him we cry "Abba, Father." The Spirit himself testifies with our spirit that we are God's children. Now if we are children, then we are heirs-heirs of God and co-heirs with Christ, if indeed we share in his sufferings in order that we may also share in his glory." Romans 8:14-17

He looked up at Jed and the old man replied, "They always like to spout off about us being sons of God, as if that makes us some kind of god ourselves. What they always leave out is verse 17. We're gonna share in his sufferings. That old viper, Peggy, may not have been too smart about the Bible references, but she sure used it against you in that meeting when she tried to make it look like you and Valerie were engaged in adultery. She was using your love for God against you. Just like it said in that Scripture we read, Psalms 22, the night that all happened. Now skip down to verse 28."

Grady read the passage:

"And we know that in all things God works for the good of those who love him, who have been called according to his purpose." Romans 8:28

"Two points here, Grady. It's *God* who does the working in those who love him, and it's for those things in which we're called *according to his purpose.* If it's not in God's purpose, it ain't gonna happen. I don't care how much faith you have or how much hollerin' you do when you pray. It isn't about getting the things we want in life or pretending we can control anything we say with our own mouth. It's God's plan that will bring us happiness. And God forbid that a man gets what he wants when it's not in God's will. A man can spend a lifetime running in circles building his own empire only to find out God wasn't in any of it. He'll only end up lonely and unhappy in the end. Look at that big, fancy preacher who we heard about in the news recently who had that glass church. He misled a whole lot of people, tellin' them it was his faith that built it. And in the end, he was bankrupt, his family was fighting over who gets to be the leader of the church and he had to sit and mourn through it all, sick and devastated, as everything he built with his own hands evaporated in front of him. I don't want to die that way. I want to pass on to be with the Lord watching my family unite around me, not fighting over a ranch or a ministry."

He repositioned himself in the rocker to turn toward Grady and grabbed his arm. "I don't want to build a church and a business up here that isn't according to the purpose of God's plan. That's why I'm not sitting down there trying to convince that bunch in front of us to do this. If it is God's will, God will show 'em. And if it *is* God's will, it might be a rough road ahead if we just let God do his part, because only God knows the best road. But one thing I can tell you is, we'll all be happy in the end, regardless of where He leads this. Are we in agreement on this, Boss?"

Grady looked up and nodded. "Yes, we are. I lived half a life watching Celia strive for things I never thought was God's will for our family. And I have to tell you, Jed, I should have been praying and being a better leader than I was for my family. God's giving me a second chance here to do it the right way. And He's given me a beautiful woman to help me do it with. She's invested a lot into my family. Missy's alive because of her. I might not have made it through the night Celia died, if it wasn't for all she did for us that night. She refused to leave my side after spending all that time in surgery fixing my little girl up. And another thing, Jed, it may not have seemed like God's will at the time, but Missy getting hurt like she did gave me something to have to deal with after Celia's death. Kept me focused for a while."

Jed asked, "So when was the point you knew you should be with Valerie?"

"I can't say I knew God wanted me to be with her until after we spent some time together. But the day she handed me this Bible, the day Missy started walking right for the first time, that was the day I knew I needed to get to know her better. She knows the Lord, and that's what drew me to her. Beauty is fleeting. But the work of the Lord stands forever."

Jed quietly sat there for a few minutes as he stared out at the cow pasture. Crissy weighed heavy on his mind. "Grady, I want you to promise me whatever happens, you'll pray before you do anything. We're about to hit rough water in a few weeks."

After Grady agreed, Jed leaned forward toward him. "Now I need to tell you something and I want your word you won't say a thing about it. Do I have your word on that, Cowboy?"

He looked back with apprehension and took in a deep breath. "I hope you're not about to tell me there are others up here who are involved in this whole scheme with the Givers. But okay! Go ahead and say what you're gonna say. I promise it will be just between us."

"The girls are coming in a few weeks because they need to talk with you. You're not gonna be happy when they get here. It's bad timing, their coming the day after the bids are read. I really didn't want them stepping into the middle of everything that's already going on right now. But they need to be with you. And right now, you need to be a leader for those three ladies. That's all I can say for now. It's not my business to be having the conversation they need to have with you."

Grady simply turned and watched the group in the pavilion, deep in thought.

Jed and Grady couldn't know it at the moment, but the road ahead and the suffering God would allow to take place, was far greater than either of them could have imagined. The dark clouds of evil which swirled over Rails End would be something no human could fix with any amount of prayer and faith. But prayer and faith would sustain them. What the men had gone through the previous year was just the training ground for a larger portion of suffering. But in the end, God would bring them through it. And in time, their tears would turn to joy.

- 9 -

THE PLEDGE

Grady awoke the next morning to a gentle touch on his shoulder, shaking him awake. As he rolled over under the soft comforter, Valerie was laying on top of it beside him. She brushed his hair back to look at his face, and said in a soft voice, "It's Sunday morning, sleepyhead. I decided to come over and fix you breakfast. It's on the table."

The fifty-two-year-old with the bushy mustache took in a deep breath as he rubbed the sleep from his eyes and smiled. "You've been baking. I only get to enjoy this kind of smell these days when I'm at Jed and Betsy's."

"You asked me to have Betsy teach me how to make her country bread recipe. Well, I bugged her enough times about it, so she came over this morning and we did a little baking in your kitchen. We were kind of surprised the smell didn't wake you up earlier. I've been here for two hours."

He gave her a kiss. "I was up pretty late. I couldn't sleep after all that discussion last night. I don't think I fell asleep until one in the morning. My conversation with Jed last night left me pretty deep in thought."

He entered the front room, showered and dressed for church. She had the table set with the nice dishes from Jed and Betsy's house. A vase of flowers sat in the center of the round table on a pretty tablecloth of sunflower patterns, with matching cloth napkins that had a bow on them. "Wow, Val. You went to a lot of trouble here!" He leaned forward and kissed her again.

They settled in at the table and he twisted his body to pop his back. "Getting older is taking a toll on me. Fifty-one isn't the same as forty-one was."

She looked down at the pretty tablecloth with a smile. "You're fifty-two Grady!" He did a double take and stared off with blinking eyes. "It's been so busy around here we blew right through your birthday, and nobody remembered it!"

"I totally forgot!"

"Well trust me! My father didn't forget. He was asking me yesterday if I was sure I wanted to marry a fifty-two-year-old man who's twenty years older than me. He said something about you being thirty-five when I was a fourteen-year-old in Junior High. He also said your wedding night will be a gift from God!" She fluttered her eyelashes at him.

He cleared his throat, staring at her for a moment. "You're ready for this, aren't you?"

She slowly nodded, "Yes, I am. I settled that issue in my mind the day I bought all those flowers for you on your fifty-first birthday. When he reminded me you were fifty-two now, I decided that deserved a nice breakfast to celebrate. Happy birthday, Grady."

The two sat through breakfast and talked as he devoured the ham omelet, thick, country bread toast and fruit salad she had prepared. He looked up hesitantly and said, "You all were deep in discussion when I left for my cabin last night. And believe me, I *am* hungry. The news about the Givers sort of ended the entire dinner before it even got started."

She quietly ate her breakfast and listened to him talk. It was only a matter of time before the conversation came around to her decision about the bid. She lifted her cloth napkin from her lap and placed her elbow on the table, parking her chin on it. "I'm sorry for being so angry last night. I really wasn't expecting to have to consider whether I wanted to tangle with that bunch who you and Jimmy ran off the ranch last year."

He looked up with apprehension in his eyes. "What was the outcome of that meeting, Val Gal? I need to know before we go any further with this entire process."

She hesitated for a moment, "I suppose you need to hear it from the boys, but they're all with you. They have a streak of hatred about those families after the lies and corruption they lived with for the last few years."

He played with his food for a few minutes before looking up again, asking, "And what about you? I'm not going forward with all of this unless we're in agreement on doing it. You're about to be my wife. That means more to me than owning this place up here. Half of what I own will belong to you."

As she started to speak, tears welled up in her eyes. "No Grady, *all* of what you own will belong to me. And all of what I own will belong to you. I'm not going to marry you without that understanding."

She stood and walked around to his side of the table. "I want you to turn and face me, Bill." As he did, she knelt on the floor in front of him, taking his hands into hers. Tears began to stream down her face as she personalized Naomi's pledge from the book of Ruth:

"Where you will go, I will go, Bill,
and where you stay, I will stay.
Your people will be my people
and your god my God.
Where you die, I will die,
and there I will be buried.
May the Lord deal with me,
be it ever so severely,
if even death separates you and me."

He looked down at her as she knelt in front of him holding hands. He lowered his body, hugging her as their faces pressed together, and began to cry. In that moment, the Lord removed a burden from his shoulders, the burden of the past and the weight of all his personal mistakes he carried about his own family.

After a long minute, as they wept together, he lifted his head and said, "You honor me, Valerie. And you do it in a way I'm not worthy of. I love you! You're such a blessing to my life!"

Jed stood on the small, four-foot by six-foot cement pad outside of the door of the Red Mill church. They watched Donavan's tall, lanky body walk up the hill as he carried his Bible. He looked up at Grady. "Well, no one else but the group who was at my house last night. One week we have fifteen, the next it's just those of us who are workin' on this old building."

"Jason's here today, Jed. That's a first! The only thing I ever saw the kid doing is drinkin' with his buddies and hanging out with that Felicia gal down in Rails End. I know what the two of them are doin' together. Let's be thankful for small gains and keep preachin' the word."

After Valerie led the group in praise songs with her guitar, Jed stood and gave the sermon.

As the service was coming to a close, he offered for anyone who wanted to talk further about living in Christ to see him after the service. Jason stepped up and asked to pray with him. "Valerie told me last night I should come today to church."

"Jason, I can't say being told to come to church is a proper reason to approach accepting Christ into your life."

Donavan leaned forward and put his hand on his shoulder. "Hear him out, Jed. That discussion last night in the pavilion was mostly about the Lord. The young man has a lot of questions. The talk about the bid and the sale of the property lasted less than fifteen minutes. The rest of us spent three hours answering his questions and talking about our testimonies."

Jason said, "Jonathon and I have been doing a lot of talking about the Bible. It seems to be the only thing he wants to discuss lately. Something changed in him. He's been happy lately ... and I can't say he has a lot of reason to be right now." The two older men shot a knowing glance at each other.

After a long pause, he looked up and stated, "I want that in my life, Jed. I'm not happy with my life. I do a lot of things I know I shouldn't. I was raised going to church, but it wasn't like what Jonathon has in his life right now."

Donny looked down at Jed with a nod of his head toward Jason and the three men got on their knees as he led the young man in a prayer of commitment to the Lord.

Afterwards, he looked up at Donavan as the two watched Jason and Jonathon walk down the hill toward the cabins. "That Jonathon's really making huge strides in the Lord, Donny. Makes me wonder?"

He looked intently at him. "Wonder about what?"

"The kid's been burning up the Scripture. He's had a lot of questions about the Lord. I've been spending time on the porch with him lately in prayer and study. He has a preacher's heart, Donny, and just brought his first convert to the Lord. How long was it before you could say that about your walk with God? I know it was a long time before it happened with me. I was too busy tryin' to figure out how to stop sinnin'." Jed looked up at him again with a wink.

- 10 -

UNCLE HANK

Hank Simons sat in his chair in the old, ranch house and stared at his nephew with his arms crossed. Jimmy argued with the elderly man as Grady sat at the old oak table watching the two, tired of the whole conversation. "Now Hank, listen to me. You all have a chance to make good on your dad's dream of owning that canyon up there. Nobody wants to move you out of the old house. I heard your Pa talking about his dream of seeing his grandsons have a better life up at Red Mill Canyon at least a dozen times before he died. Now the opportunity is here. And Grady ain't asking, Hank. He owns the entire Acreage. All he wants is your approval."

Grady got up from his chair and drug it over to his uncle's side. "Uncle Hank, Grandpa talked about it, my dad talked about it, and now the chance is here. I know you weren't happy with me going up to work for the bunch who own Red Mill last year. And I surely never thought at the time the opportunity would come. But it has and I'll never see the chance of having it happen again in my lifetime. Surely not in your lifetime, you old buzzard."

Hank crossed his arms, "Do what you're gonna do. You never listened to me in the past, anyway."

He looked down and shook his head. "It ain't about the land, Uncle Hank. It's not even about the dream your dad had." He looked up. "It's about the wedding." He stood up and walked across the room to the kitchen and started making a pot of coffee.

He watched his nephew from a distance as Jimmy stared out the window toward the beauty of the plains. "So, what's so important about this wedding anyway, boy? I was at the first one. Loved that Celia. Always did! She was good to me, Billy Boy. Always took time to visit me and never failed to bring me a cake when she did it."

He leaned on the counter and stared for a moment at the elderly man. "That whole tizzy fit you threw last year, that was about Celia, wasn't it?" He walked back over to him and sat in the chair. Hank wiped his nose and his eyes. "I'm sorry, Uncle Hank. I loved Celia and I know she was your favorite. You treated her just as well as she treated you. She loved you, old man."

He looked off at the window as his elderly uncle got up from his chair and walked across the kitchen, pouring himself a cup of coffee. He returned to his seat, took a sip and stared at the two men. "So, tell me, boy. What's so important about this wedding?"

He looked up, wiping his own eyes now. "Hank, you're the only one left in your family. My dad can't be here to take part in the wedding. I just figured that..." *and his voice trailed off for a moment.* "Hank, you're the only man in the family who I've got left now. You're the only one I have to look up to. I just wanted you to be there. That's all! I came out here today because we ain't been talkin' long enough now."

Grady looked down and spoke a little quieter. "I guess I thought if anyone could appreciate this whole idea of owning the canyon again, it would be you. And the goings on down here in the future would be a real ranch again. Just like the old days. Let's face it. Those Givers sorta' outsmarted themselves. We have a chance to own the canyon *and* the Acreage now. And the value of this ranch and the two houses will back most of the loan, Hank. This is the best spread in the meadows. The land's worth more than any other property. Especially when you add in all the cattle. Maybe the operations are contracted out these days, but the herd belongs to us. So do the farming operations out in the north forty."

Jimmy turned back from the window, looking the old man in the eyes. "Hank, your boys never wanted the ranch. They all work at the plant. You know Bill was the one who carried it all on after your dad and your brother passed on. You can die knowing the dream your dad had is alive and happening right outside your window every day. Just like the past, Hank."

"Go ahead and do it, boy. And when it's said and done, I don't want to ever see a Giver or a Smith on any of our property again. You don't so much as rent a cabin to 'em or sell a side of beef to 'em in the future, Bill. You give me your word on that, son!"

He looked down and laughed with a shake of his head. "Believe me Hank. As soon as this deal's done, I won't so much as ever speak to a Giver or a Smith for as long as I live." He looked up at him. "And the wedding?"

"I'll be there, Billy. And I want my own cabin up there! It's been too long. I want to see Red Mill Canyon as soon as this is finished. Lord knows you'll have enough of those cabins up there to spare one."

He got a broad grin on his face which accentuated his large, handlebar mustache. "You'll have your own place up there. And you're gonna like this gal, Hank. She's a great woman. When she looks at Sonrisa, it's just like watchin' your dad when he looked at it. She loves the place more than I do. And let's not forget Celia never graced that swimming hole once in thirty years. Val makes me take her up to the old, swimming hole every weekend. You're gonna like the girl. I promise!"

"So, what's so important about this trip the two of you are taking today? What's going on, Billy?"

Jimmy turned away and looked out the window as Grady gave his uncle a grimace. "You just leave that to me. It's best not to say anything about that. Let's just say we plan to make good on that gimp arm of yours." He stood and bent over his uncle, giving him a hug.

Hank watched the two as they gathered their stuff. "Billy, I have a question for you. I was sitting in Drakes Hardware the other day with my son. The five of you *Mulligans* carved your names on a wood beam up above the register area when you were youngins."

Jimmy was in the middle of standing and froze, staring at the floor like a deer in the headlights. It was the first time he had heard the name *Mulligans* in over thirty-five years. He slowly lifted his chin to look at Grady with a solid, piercing stare. Grady just returned the stare, remaining silent for a long moment. He cocked his head toward the door and said, "Go on outside. I'll catch up."

He stared at Hank, waiting till Jimmy was well off the porch. "Why're you even bringing this up in front of Jimmy? That was stupid! Nothing's changed about this since we were kids."

"I was just wondering if you've ever heard from her?"

He took a stance with his hands on his hips, staring at Hank for several seconds. "Jimmy don't want to talk about Cass and neither do I." He stared off through the window with an exasperated look. "Look … Hank, for many years we struggled through what happened to the Jacksons and Cass both. For some reason, we couldn't get beyond Cass being torn from our lives and it caused a lot of hard feelings between the four of us, so we agreed not to talk about her. He lost his parents! Ya' don't start digging holes in a cemetery! You know what I mean? Don't bring this up again when Jimmy's in the room." As he stood there, staring at him, he snorted out a quiet laugh, "Mulligans! How did you even remember that name?"

"I'm the first one who called you kids by that name."

He stared at him for a moment and said, "I didn't know that." He looked through the open door to see Jimmy leaning back against the front grill of his truck, angrily staring at him with his arms crossed. He looked at Hank again and said, "Just … let dead dogs lie, old man."

He turned and walked through the door and off the porch, heading across the dirt toward the truck. Jimmy just stood there, staring at him with his arms crossed. As he passed him, he said, "He's getting old. And he has no clue what we discussed the day we burned the cabin down." As he pulled the driver's door open, he stood for a moment and watched Jimmy still leaning back against the truck. "Do you ever think about her?"

Jimmy turned quickly, looking at him. "Oh, I *think* about her! But the thoughts I have about her are probably not the same kind of thoughts *you* have about her!"

He leaned against the open window frame of the door with both arms on it as they stared at each other. "Any way I respond to that is just gonna piss you off even more. Just get in the truck."

He slid into the driver's seat as Jimmy walked around to his door and opened it, sliding onto the seat. "Just once! I would like you to at least consider taking my side on this just once!"

Grady quickly threw the door open and stepped away from the truck. He turned and yelled, **"I quit defending her the day we burned the Cassmore cabin down! Nothing has changed!"** He turned away from the truck and watched the livestock. He finally turned back to the truck and said, "It's been twenty-five years since we've mentioned her name, but you're just as raw about it as you were then! I didn't bring this up. Hank did! Don't go there with me, Jimmy! I loved the girl just as much as you did! I just don't hate her the way you do because of what her father did! There hasn't been a year gone by I haven't wished you weren't the one who found their bodies, Jimmy!" He turned away for a moment and bit his lip, looking off across the pastureland.

Jimmy said, "I'm sorry. Just … just get in the truck."

Grady slid in and slammed the door. He stared at Jimmy and said, "I'm sorry. There's just a lot going on right now and the last thing I need is discissions of Cass and what her father did coming up in the middle of this."

Jimmy sat quietly as he put the truck in gear and drove off. He smiled at him and said, "Mulligans! I forgot all about that name." Grady smiled at him and both men burst out laughing.

Grady slowed in the chortling truck at the end of the dirt driveway as they stared at the estate house which sat in the middle of the Acreage. He drove by slowly as they looked out the window. "She sure is a beauty, Billy. We had some great times in that old place, didn't we?"

"We sure did spend a lot of time helping my dad fix that place up and adding onto it when my grandfather turned the whole thing over to him. Never understood why my wife didn't want to live in that house after my mom passed a few years ago. Three stories and a swimming pool to boot. She just wanted to be in the place on snob hill. Never understood why. It was only half the size of this place. I have to admit, it was one of the nicest houses on the street. Celia sure did have a knack for picking out show pieces."

As the two men turned off Simmons Drive onto Shaker Road, Grady looked back in his rear-view mirror. "There they are, Jimmy, just like you said. They sat and waited there for us the whole time." The two men headed out to the Meadowlands expressway toward the desert basin and stopped at the Gas Mart to fill up the truck. Grady put on his cowboy hat and coat, glancing at Jared Brine's old Buick, which had pulled off the road down the highway.

He stepped out, put the gas nozzle in the truck and started filling it. He went into the bathroom and Donavan was standing there, leaning on the sink with a broad smile on his face. "Are they following you?"

He grinned, "Dumber than a bunch of goats, Donny. They're sitting down the road a ways in that dented old Buick of Jared's." He pulled the coat and hat off, handing them to the man. "Don't forget to pull the gas nozzle out before you drive off."

"How did you know they would be following you around today? Honestly, I thought my driving out here would be a waste of time."

"Jimmy's idea! He said if they were planning something, they would be watching us this week. He also said if they did watch us, whatever they have planned could be bad."

"Define *bad* for me!"

He put his hands in the air with a shrug. "Explain to me what makes a family want to run a bar that draws in all of the lowlifes in town and maybe I can give you an intellectual assessment of Rails End's most notable scum. I don't spend my life thinking like a crook or hanging out with them."

Donavan said, "The Brines and the Jenkins aren't the smartest families in town. It's the Givers who worry me. They act and dress like bankers, but for forty years, they've had their hands in all of the problem issues in the entire Meadows Region. And if you need me to define that for you, then talk to your uncle Hank. He only has one arm that works because of that family. And what concerns me more is they got away with it when it happened the first time."

He looked down at the tile floor with a quiet demeanor as Donavon put on the hat and coat. The skinny, tall cowboy stuck his hand out and waited. He looked up at him and asked, "What?"

"I just thought if you're giving me your hat and coat, then maybe you'd give me your credit card, as well."

"No!" As Donavan started laughing, Grady replied, "The credit card comes with the boots, Donny. The day you get my boots, I won't need the credit card anymore."

Donavan jumped into the Super Duty with Jimmy and the two drove off down the highway. He came out of the bathroom and watched his truck depart as Jared Brine pulled out and passed the Gas Mart, keeping a distance from the truck. Grady smiled and shook his head. "Idiots! Nothing but a bunch of idiots."

He waited for a few minutes, buying a cup of coffee, and then went outside and jumped in Donavan's new Dodge Dually, heading down the highway in the opposite direction toward Los Angeles.

- 11 -

SOUTHLAND SUMMIT

Grady listened to the smooth, declining whine of the truck's transmission as the large, four-door Dodge diesel truck came down the exit ramp and escaped the busy 110 Freeway to the light at Olympic. He turned left and made his way through the high-rise district and continued to the seedier side of downtown Los Angeles. The cowboy drove around the collection of buildings in the garment district and peered down Santee Alley as he drove by a few times, looking at the instructions on his small sheet of paper, searching for a good place to park.

He exited his truck, strolling down the collection of small shops in the unique shopping venue which ran for a city block down the alley, stopping to look at a few items in the store fronts and booths as he looked at his watch. After a half-hour of shopping and three new scarves for Valerie, he headed back up the alley to the hotdog restaurant near the corner, watching for familiar faces. When he didn't see any, he slipped into the small shop which was filled with confections, drinks and a hot dog grill. He smiled, "At least the man knows what a cowboy likes to eat."

He stepped up to the counter and said, "Give me three of those hot dogs. All beef with everything on them."

The woman at the register turned and called out, "Pelon!"

The man at the grill eyed the tall cowboy with the tan hat and said, "I'll take this one, Chica." He took his money and asked, "Do you have a discount card?"

Grady laid his wallet on the counter and opened it so the man could see his sheriff's badge, and picked it up and flipped it shut, putting it back in his pocket.

"Joshy!" he called out, motioning his head toward the door. The teenager put the empty trays on the kitchen counter and walked out to the front of the business, pulling a cigarette out and lighting it as he sat on a large, cement planter and looked up and down the walkway and small courtyard in front. After the man put the order on the red plastic tray and pushed it toward Grady, he looked up at the young man out front, who threw his cigarette on the ground and crushed it. Josh locked eyes with the business owner and shook his head.

Juan Martinez motioned toward the walkway through the kitchen and Grady lifted the tray and followed. They passed through the hallway which was stacked with boxes and Grady surveyed the busy place, watching the workers carrying cases into the large walk-in door. Juan pushed the dirty backdoor of the kitchen open, shoving the screen, and led him to a patio corridor outside. "Have a seat. Mr. Thomas will be here soon enough. We're the only ones who come out here after the morning suppliers are done. It's safe."

"Nice little patio, my friend."

"I have a wife. She keeps the gardening up in the pots and planters. We started out running a gardening business. I don't let a lot of people know about the patio. The Thomas' are one of the few who we let use it."

"How did you go from gardening to running a restaurant?"

"It was a dream. We all have dreams. I used to do all the gardening for the Thomas family. Mr. Thomas took a liking to me, for some reason. When this place came open, he helped me get it started. I let him use the patio whenever he needs it. Normally I don't even charge him when he has a meeting here, but he was very specific about not drawing any attention this time, so I let you pay for your meal."

He started to give an explanation and Juan put his hands in the air, "I don't need to know. Mr. Thomas' business is his business. He's a good man, Mr. Simmons." Grady raised his eyebrows as he heard the man say his name and Juan said, "I looked at your license when you flipped the wallet on the counter. It *is* Simmons, right?" He nodded and Juan shook his hand. "I have orders on the grill. I have to get back inside." The man turned and went in the door.

A few minutes later Doug Thomas Sr. came through the door to the patio carrying two trays and sat with a smile. "So, we finally meet! Dougy has good things to say about you, Mr. Simmons. Frankly, I wish you would have shown up in Red Mill a lot sooner than you did. It might have saved all of us a lot of grief. That place has been nothing but problems for my family this year."

The ranch manager cleared his throat, pushing the tray aside, "For both of us!"

"What makes a railroad man decide to suddenly leave his job and take over a ranch, if you don't mind my asking?"

"My family once owned a third of Red Mill Canyon. I was in a place to take an early retirement. My family has run cattle for many years. But Red Mill is where all of that started. I just wanted to be up on the ranch. I have a lot of great childhood memories about the place."

"And now you want to own it! And so do the Givers! Tell me more about this change in life you suddenly decided to put yourself through. Was it because of your wife's passing?"

His mouth opened slightly as he stared back at the lawyer in the three-piece suit. He struggled to answer the question and Mr. Thomas could see the sudden agitation in his face. "Mr. Simmons, let me make one thing clear here. In the last year my family has had seven lawsuits filed against us from other owners in the Red Mill Association. I decided to make it my business to know as much as I could about everyone up there. And that goes for your young surgeon, as well. After finding out Ron's, Darcy's and Peggy's families are all related, I'm not in a very trusting position. Right now, I don't know if we're being played from two sides or if you're really their enemy. I've been in the legal business for many years, and I've seen a lot of things no one would believe. Right now, you have me sitting with you and talking, so that should tell you a lot about which way I'm leaning in all of this."

He sat up straight in his chair, "You're preachin' to the choir here, Mr. Thomas! Do you know Mac Grady?"

"I know him. His dad and I were on the board together in the early days of the Red Mill Association. I liked him. The two of us had to sort out a lot of things when we started the Association. We spent the first five years having our Christmas vacations on the ranch with our families."

"Talk to Mac Grady. He's one of my best friends. We grew up together. He, Sheriff Jackson and his brother Johnny and I all grew up together. Our families were very close. If you trust Mac, he'll vouch for me."

"You left out a name in that group you just mentioned." Grady's face had a questioning look and the lawyer said, "Cassmore! Their daughter ran with your group of friends."

His mouth fell open wide and his upper body swayed slightly from side-to-side in disbelief. This was the second time in one day someone was mentioning Cass. Grady breathed in hard and stood from the bench and grabbed his phone and cowboy hat, putting it on.

He turned to head to the door and stopped abruptly as Jennifer Thomas stood in front of him. "Hear my dad out. He has good reason for being so skeptical, Mr. Simmons. Everyone in my family knows you worked hard to root out what was taking place on the ranch last year. We just want the lawsuits to stop. The three families being related was something we didn't know about."

"What does the *Cassmore* family have to do with any of that?" he angrily intoned. "And where's Doug? I thought Doug was going to be here!"

"Doug's the president of the Association. He's in charge of the committee who's selling the property. It's a huge conflict of interest for him to be sitting with you right now having private meetings." After ten seconds of silence Jennifer pointed at his chair, "Take a seat, Mr. Simmons. Hear my father out. He just wants to be sure that what you know is what our investigators have found out. He's your friend, not your enemy."

"Then why bring up the name Cassmore! That happened nearly forty years ago!" He sat back down on the bench and took his hat off with an angry look.

Mr. Thomas folded his hands, leaning on the table. "I apologize, Mr. Simmons. I shouldn't have brought up the Cassmore memory and thrown it in your face like that. Horace Grady and I did a lot of business together when we were in the early days of the Association. I know about all of the things which took place back forty years ago. Horace and I talked about it. And to answer your question, the Cassmore and the Jackson families have nothing to do with it. All four of their parents are dead now. You ... brought up the Jacksons, so I just wanted to make it clear I knew as much about the past as you do." As he watched Grady's reaction intently, he stated, "She's alive, you know that, right?"

He pursed his lips together tightly, pressing his fore finger hard in the groove of his lips as he leaned his chin into his hand, staring off at the flowering planter behind the table. He finally lifted both hands in the air and shook his head slowly. "Winnifred? We're talking about Winnifred Cassmore here. Right? Last I heard she was alive. Mac talked to her several years back. Aside from that, I don't know anything about her. I haven't seen her for ... for ..."

Jennifer softly said, "Thirty-six years."

"You two are something else! I came here to talk about the Giver's, the Brine's and the Jenkins' families. Winnifred Cassmore has nothing to do with all of this!"

She turned in her seat and was about to answer the question when her father patted her hand as it lay on the table. He stated, "That's exactly what we wanted to hear. Let's just move on from that. She really has no bearing on what's going on now."

She kept a straight face through the rest of the conversation as Douglas Sr. and Grady talked out what the ranch manager knew and what he heard in the Cougar Lounge a few weeks back. A half-hour later, Grady stood and shook their hands and was about to leave. Douglas asked, "Mr. Simmons, before you leave, I have a favor to ask of you. The man who owns this restaurant, he used to be my gardener." As Grady nodded, Mr. Thomas stated, "One of his sons still does gardening and he wants out of L.A. Juan wants him out of L.A. The man has kept his son out of the kinds of problems that drag some of the migrants in this area down. He's a great gardener. If you're awarded the bid on the ranch, are you planning on hiring a gardener?"

"Probably. I haven't gotten down to the finer details of who we need to hire."

"I'd like you to consider the young man for a job. He wants to move up to the Sierras. Can I have him come up and meet you? I can vouch for the family. I've known Juan and his kids for several years. The young man's about twenty-five and has a wife and two kids. We call him Poncho."

Grady put his hat on his head, "Send the man up to meet me. You have my phone number. If he shows up for an interview, I'll know he's serious about wanting a job."

He turned and headed for the door. Jennifer and Mr. Thomas stared at each other for a moment, and she asked, "Why didn't you tell him more about Cassmore's daughter?"

Doug breathed in hard, "I just needed to know how much he knew about her. It was a test. I needed to know if he's a friend or an enemy. When you get someone mad because you throw a curve ball at them that's a soft spot, it sort of resets the whole conversation. I also wanted to know if he likes her or hates her like the rest of the town does."

"Well, you got your answer on that one, Daddy. It was a bad memory!"

Doug smiled back at his daughter, "No Jenny, what happened *thirty-six years ago* is a bad memory. But the man cares about her. He felt trapped when I forced him to talk about her. He's conflicted. On one side of his thoughts, she was a young woman who he cared deeply about. On the other side of his thoughts, he has no desire to dredge up the entire history of what happened thirty-six years ago. He was mad enough about my bringing it up that if he hated her, he would have made it very clear. Instead, he just wanted out of the conversation."

"So why didn't you tell him more about her?"

He stood, grabbing his red plastic, food tray, "It's nobody's business knowing about Winnifred Cassmore and where she is. The woman is doing fine today. Horace Grady made that clear to me when I setup her and her mother's arrangements over thirty years ago. He told me Bill, the Jackson boys and his son didn't need to know any more about her than he wanted them to know. If Miss Cassmore wants them to know anything, she'll let them know. And trust me on this, you don't want to get on her bad side. The woman wields a lot of influence these days." He nodded toward the door, "I've already said more than I should have. Let's just forget about Winnifred and move on. There's a reason I keep that file locked up in my safe at home."

Grady slid into the large, Dodge truck and shut the door. He stared out the windshield for a minute and tears flooded his eyes. He whispered, *"How did Cass get drug into all of this? The last thing I wanted to talk about was Winnifred Cassmore. Everyone needs to just bury the memory and let her live in peace."*

It had been twenty-five years since he had even had a conversation about her, other than talking with Valerie about the names carved on the tree on the North rim the previous year. Grady, Mac, and the Jackson's had agreed to never bring her name up again. Now her name had come up twice in one day. He lifted his phone and very rapidly typed out a text. *"I just met with Doug Thomas' father. I'm leaving L.A. Why is this lawyer asking me about Cass? What does she have to do with all of this business up at the ranch?"*

Mac Grady stood from his lunch table at the Roadhouse

Restaurant, shaking hands with Jimmy Jackson and Burl Avery as the town sheriff put his Mounty style hat on and walked to the bar to talk with his brother, Johnny. He zipped his briefcase and grabbed his cell phone as it started buzzing on the table. He stood as he moved his thumb around on the keyboard while he lifted his briefcase, opening the text message from Grady. *"I just met with Doug Thomas' father. I'm leaving L.A. Why is this lawyer asking me about Cass? What does she have to do with all of this business up at the ranch?"*

He suddenly froze, dropping his briefcase to the floor and flopping down in his seat again with a worried look. The businessman sat and stared at the screen for a very long time before looking up at the Jacksons as they talked at the long, western-style bar at the end of the room.

He started to type, *"She's alive. I know she's living ...."* He deleted the words. He started typing again, *"My Dad was her overse..."* He stared at the screen before deleting the message again.

He sat back with his head hanging back over the wooden, dining room chair and stared up at the ceiling rafters and the western chandelier above his table. His heart pounded heavily as he meditated on what to tell him and what needed to be kept secret about Winnie Cassmore. Mac's father had been her caretaker after her parents had died. Horace Grady had transferred the responsibility to him before he had died. He finally sat up and typed, *"She has nothing to do with it. Do us both a favor and just move on from this. Mr. Thomas and my dad did a lot of business together in the early days. He should have kept anything about Cassmore, and what happened, to himself. Don't discuss this with Johnny and Jimmy. We agreed to move on from this a long time ago, Billy. It will just cause problems if you talk about her."*

- 12 -

PARADISE GAINED

Two weeks later, the entire board of the ranch faced a packed meeting hall as the buyers sat in small groups in the audience, waiting for the meeting to start. One-by-one, Grady and Valerie watched the audience of people walk through the door. The entire ranch staff was present, as well as several people who they knew from town. Reverend Spicer sat in the back of the hall praying, and the publisher of the Ledger sat with a reporter in the front row taking notes.

Burl Avery, the owner and publisher of the Daily Ledger, spent the past year milking the stories about the arrest and the trials of Peggy Withers, Joe Brine and Darcy Jenkins. It was the biggest news to hit Rails End in years, other than the expansion of the Harville mining operations to Furline Canyon. Lately, the struggle to expand the rail lines through the Meadowlands was taking the top of the fold on the front of the paper. The Ledger, which had recently added Sunday morning to their delivery, was riding a wave of popularity in the last year and the newspaper was expanding rapidly due to the increased readership.

What had taken place on the ranch, the oldest institution in the entire Meadows region, was a treasure trove of news that just kept on giving, as the lawsuits were filed, and the ownership had become divided. It had become a real mess and the Ledger had covered every meeting and court room motion throughout the winter and on into spring. For Burl Avery, the combination of a Sunday edition and the sudden flow of local news about Red Mill and Furline Canyon were a grand slam for the small, hometown paper.

Dr. Mansfield had even made the drive up the North Fork Road to sit with Valerie and Grady for the announcement. As Doug Thomas III stood up to the podium and started the meeting, you could hear a pin drop with all the silence and anticipation that filled the entire hall.

Doug gave a short speech, as was his style of grandeur when standing before such a large group, drawing the proceeding out. Someone yelled from the back of the hall, **"Just get on with it, Dougy!"** followed by laughter and giggles from all across the room.

He opened the envelope and announced with a loud voice, "The winning bid goes to Bill Simmons, Jed Gentry and Donavan Rice!" The entire ranch staff jumped to their feet and cheered while Grady and Valerie stood, hugging each other, surrounded by the group. Grady looked on at Jack Jenkins, who pulled his cell phone from his pocket and stormed out of the hall. The ranch manager smiled back at Jed and Donavan. *"Good riddance to you all!"* he muttered under his breath as Jack walked out.

Jed looked at him with a huge smile, "Well done, Grady!" and the three men shook hands. They walked to the board table and all three prepared to sign the documents. But at that very moment, Betsy and Valerie scurried up and interrupted the group. She lifted a velvet-covered pen box from her pocket, handing it to her fiancé. Inside the blue box was a gold pen with an inscription etched into it. He looked at the pen closely and read the simple words on the side. "For Grandfather!" He choked up emotionally as he passed the pen to the others to see.

"Betsy and I thought it would be the right thing to do." They watched as each man took turns signing the documents with the pen. Doug Thomas took the pen and turned to her. "First Class, Dr. Dobbins!" and signed the documents. He passed the pen to each board member to use when they signed the agreement. Doug shook their hands and said, "In three days, we transfer the deed to the property down at the Meadowlands Title Company." The entire group cheered again when the signatures were all on the documents.

Betsy grabbed Grady's face in her hands and said, "Valerie and I made up some party fixins' over at your cabin while you were gone yesterday. Jed and I have something appropriate to share with y'all. I had the boys put some chairs out on your porch. Let's go over to your place and celebrate, Cowboy."

When everyone filed out of the hall, no one took notice of Mac Grady, from the Grady Corporation, sitting in a chair in the corner of the hall. He was watching everything taking place with a brooding look as he quietly sat there. Mac was an owner in the Association. His ownership was small peanuts in light of the other holdings he owned and operated, but his childhood friend, Grady, winning the bid for future ownership of the ranch was something he was concerned about. Mac had brought some men up to the ranch who were busy during the meeting, unbeknownst to anyone in attendance. And for now, it was his secret.

Grady, Jed, and Donavan sat on the porch and talked about the plans for the future of the ranch while Valerie helped Betsy serve the food. The two women sat a large pie on the small table in the center of the porch and placed a bowl of fried chicken and veggies with ranch dip on the table. As the men filled their plates and took a seat, Valerie sat on the swing, lifting her legs and tucking her feet under her lap, leaning into Grady's large shoulder, watching everyone eat as they celebrated.

Betsy brought a gift box out with a large, tattered bow on the top, handing it to Jed. He opened the lid, sliding a tall bottle of cognac from the box. "Old man Stevens gave this to us fifteen years ago. It was our twenty-fifth wedding anniversary. We've had it in the liquor cabinet in the cabin house. We just figured that someday we would have a good reason to unwrap the seal on this old bottle and pull the cork. It just seemed fitting that a gift from the man who did more to build this ranch than anybody in the past was the appropriate thing to share at the moment."

Jed unwrapped the metal seal, pulling it off the top and tapped the cork with the corkscrew on his Swiss army knife, working it out. He took a swig off the bottle and handed it to Betsy. "Oh Jed!" she said with a bit of embarrassment and hesitated, before putting the bottle to her mouth. She handed the bottle to Donavan, and he passed it around the circle as each person put the bottle to their lips and took a swig.

Grady handed the heavy bottle to Valerie and said, "I don't think you better pass on this one, Val Gal!" She looked on with hesitation and finally lifted the bottle to her lips and took a small sip. As she grimaced, she handed the bottle back to him and swallowed hard. "That's nasty! How do you guys drink this stuff?" The entire group started clapping.

After the others left, she turned over onto Grady's lap and laid her head against his chest. He wrapped his arms around her body and held her, as the swing rocked back and forth. She smiled up at him. "Congratulations, Grady. This is a pretty big month for you."

"No, Val. This is pretty big month for *us*! And we haven't even gotten to the best part, yet."

Tomorrow was Wednesday and neither of them could imagine just how wrong the statement would turn out to be. But for the moment, ignorance was bliss as they rocked on the swing.

At the very same moment, the Brines, Givers and Jenkins stood in Jack Jenkins garage, wearing dark clothing as they loaded their shotguns.

- 13 -

THE BURNINGS OF AUGUST!

Grady stomped his boots hard as he walked across the porch of the Gentry cabin, pulling the screen on the door open. Betsy was cooking in the kitchen while Jed sat in his chair at the head of the table, sipping his coffee and reading the Ledger. He held the paper up to display the bold headline in large print. "**Red Mill Canyon Goes To The Staff !!!**"

"There it is business partner. Everyone in town's reading it right about now! How's it feel to be an owner up here?"

He smiled broadly and walked to the kitchen, pouring himself a cup of coffee. The two men sat at the table, reading and re-reading the article. "We need to cut this one out, Jed. It's the first thing about the ranch, for months, that hasn't been trailer-park trash in this paper!"

Betsy brought out the plates, as the bacon cooked on the cast iron griddle in the kitchen. He looked up at her, "Where'd Val go this morning? She sure was up early. She's usually not up for a good hour yet."

Jed lowered the paper and she stopped putting plates down as they both stared back at him. "Valerie's still sleeping in the guest room."

"No, she's not. She took my truck out to do something. It was gone when I came out this morning." Jed chuckled and kept reading the paper as Betsy stared back at him with a puzzled look.

"Valerie's asleep, Cowboy! She told me to wake her at eight o'clock. She was reading in the sofa chair till midnight."

Jed lowered the paper again and the two men looked at each other. Grady stood and walked down the hallway, pushing the door of the guest room open. He stared at the big lump under the comforter. He sat on the bed and pulled the covers back to reveal her face with a mess of brown hair covering it.

"Graaadddy!" she said with a groggy voice, pulling the covers back over her head. "What are you doing? I don't have to be at the clinic till noon today. I'm not ready to get up yet!" She pulled the covers back, smiling at him. "And no peeking at my jammies for three weeks yet, old man." She pulled the covers back over her head.

He rolled his eyes and just sat there for a moment thinking this through. She shifted under the comforter and said, **"What is with you!"** kicking at him, very annoyed now.

"Valerie, where's my truck? Did you use it last night? It's not in front of my cabin."

She pulled the covers back, "Now get serious, Bill! When have I ever driven that big truck without you in it? You know I don't like driving it. Go talk to Donavan. I saw him driving it in town a few days ago."

He stood to face Jed and Betsy, who were standing at the door. "Something's not right here, Jed." He pushed his way past the two and quickly left the cabin.

He jumped into the Polaris and quickly drove down the road past the meadow toward the barn. He banged on the door of the bunk house till Jason opened it. "Sorry. It's usually unlocked. What's up, Boss?"

"Where's Donny? I need to talk to him!" Grady demanded.

Jonathon came out of the bathroom in a tee shirt with shaving cream on this face. "Donny's across the way in the maintenance shed. I just talked to him a few minutes ago."

"Donny's truck isn't here. He must have gone somewhere." He turned, quickly walking across the road to the shed. He threw the door open and stared at the tall mechanic with a look of panic. "Donny, where's our trucks?"

"Mine's next to my cabin. I don't have a clue where yours is."

"No, Donny! Yours is gone. Mine is also missing!" He looked across the street to the two men standing on the stoop of the bunk house. "Wake everyone up and get 'em down here. We're calling a meeting right now."

Grady and Donavan talked in front of the shed while the staff assembled in a huddle around the two men. "Mine and Donny's trucks are gone. Does anyone know about this?" The staff simply looked on, dumfounded.

Jed stared back with a look of concern, "I think the bell just rang for round two! We heard them say, if we won the bid on the ranch, they were gonna do something."

He paced around for a minute as everyone watched. Valerie stepped toward him, to talk to him, and suddenly shrank back as he picked up a heavy wrench from the greasy maintenance table nearby. He flung it hard against the metal door of the garage with a loud growl, putting a huge dent in the door. He paced back and forth in front of the garage and ran a hand through his hair.

Jed walked up to him and said, "Grady, what did we agree on? You're scaring everyone. We need to pray right here and right now, boy!" Jed called the group over and they held hands as he led them in prayer, asking for God's guidance and protection.

No sooner had they finished praying when Grady's phone rang, announcing, *"Sheriff Jackson"*. "Billy, this is Jimmy. I need you to come to the substation. One of my officers found two trucks at the bottom of the river at the North Fork Bridge. She says the trucks belong to you and Donavan Rice. They were driven off the curve right before the bend to the bridge. There isn't much left of them, Bill. It's a pretty far drop to the river there. Meet Officer Jernigan on your way down. She's there now."

"Get in the Polaris, Donny. They found our trucks at the bridge. Someone ran 'em off a cliff!"

Grady and Donavan stood on the side of the road as a line of cars from the ranch pulled up while they were looking down at the wreckage at the bottom of the river canyon. Donavan just shook his head as Jonathon looked over the edge of the cliff, while Grady talked to the officer. "That just ain't right, Donavan!" the young man muttered as he looked down on the wreckage.

After a few minutes, Grady returned to the group. "Donny, you and I need to take a ride down to Rails End. Jonathon, take the Polaris back up to the ranch. Jed, why don't you bring the ladies down with you and meet us? We're gonna need a ride back up and we're gonna need to pick up Valerie's truck."

As the two men rode down the highway with Officer Jernigan, she turned and said, "I pretty much wondered if things were going to get out of hand, now that you won the bid last night. I've seen a lot of dirty tricks with that group the Jenkins run with. They're all a bunch of crooks and hoodlums. And I know about them all being related. Sheriff Jackson briefed us on that the other day. It pretty much draws most of the families together who we have problems with down in Rails End. If it isn't drinking and fighting, it's something else with all three of those families." Grady and Donavan just looked out their respective windows in silence.

A few minutes later the radio on the police cruiser crackled and the dispatcher called out, **"24, respond."**

She picked up the mic and replied, "24!"

"Patsy, get to the Simmons ranch. Don't come to the office. Is Bill with you?"

"10-4!"

The dispatcher said, "Man ... okay! What's said is already said. Just get him over to his dad's place right away." As she spoke, they could hear a hive of confusion in the office with sirens in the background. A few minutes later the radio began to sound off as other officers began rapidly talking.

Grady and Donavan sat up straight as they stared at the radio. Sheriff Jackson's voice rang out, **"I want everyone on Tac-Two!"** She looked up at Grady with concern.

"What's Tac-Two?" he asked.

"It's the tactical channel. It means we're gearing up to have a gun battle or something's going down that's really bad." She switched the dial on the radio.

Jackson's voice bellowed out, **"21 take the south road. 27 take the ranch road. Nobody gets in or out of there unless it's a squad car or a first responder. Dispatch, call Temple Ridge and tell them we need back up in town. I have everyone on this. 24, ETA?"**

She picked up the mic and said, "Twenty minutes. Two C. R."

After a short pause, Sheriff Jackson's voice bellowed out again. **"Bill and Donavan, or is it Bill and Dr. Dobbins?"**

"Bill and Donavan, Boss."

He quietly cussed and keyed off the mic for a second. After a brief pause, he spoke again. **"Billy, I know you can hear me right now so I'm just gonna say it! It's a mess out on the Acreage. They burned your Daddy's house and killed all the livestock!"**

Grady gasped as Donavan grabbed the back of the seat, pulling himself forward. "What?!"

"Look Bill, I have a unit at Uncle Hank's place right now. He's hurt and in pretty bad shape. I should know more by the time you get here." As Sheriff Jackson spoke, the three of them could hear a siren scream past him.

"Patsy. I need you to be on your toes when you get out here. I might need you to do a T. C. I'll have back up for you when you arrive. Do you understand what I mean, Patsy?"

After a long hesitation, she shook her head and pressed the mic. "Yeah, Jimmy ... I know what you mean. 10-4."

She pulled the cruiser over to the side of the road and looked at him. "Are you alright, Bill?"

He stared at her with a look of pain and tears streaming down his face. "Just get me to Hank's house, Patsy!"

She touched his arm, "I need you to promise me you'll restrain yourself when we get there, Bill. Can you do that? It's going to be bad, and I need to know I can trust you. Jimmy just gave me orders to take you into custody if you get out of hand. I don't want to do that, Bill, but I will if I have to."

He looked at her and nodded his head. She turned and said, "Donavan, Mr. Gentry just pulled up behind us. I need you to go tell them what's going on. Dr. Dobbins needs to stay in his vehicle till we get there. Tell him to just follow us."

As the cruiser pulled onto Shaker Road which bordered the Acreage, the fire lit up the early, dawn sky. Smoke was thickly billowing at the center of the ranch. Patsy looked toward Grady, who held his hand over his mouth with a look of horror on his face. The entire scene was punctuated by flashing lights in the distance which played against the thick smoke. Patsy stopped her vehicle in front of the police cruiser which had a barricade across the dirt road that led to the center of the ranch between the fenced-in pastureland. "Let the truck in that's behind us, Joey," she yelled out the window to the officer at the barricade, who was moving it to let her pass.

Donavan put his hand on his shoulder as the three looked across the pastureland which was riddled with the corpses of dead cows. The entire livestock, on both sides of the road, had been shot. Grady grabbed the hair on the top of his head and pulled down hard on it as he looked down at his lap, hiding his grief. Jernigan stared with her mouth open wide. "Who would do such a thing?" she said with a shocked look.

Donavan put both hands on his boss's shoulders and comforted him. "Be still, my friend, and just pray. Turn it to the Lord. We made preparations."

He looked up and turned with a fire in his eyes. **"Not for this, Donny! The value of the house and the cattle were backing that loan, as well as our trucks! The trucks alone were worth $150,000! They were both new!"**

Patsy pulled the car over and stopped, putting her hand on his arm. "Bill…" but she sat there silent for a moment. "There's no use in going to your dad's house. We need to get to Hank's house. Try to be calm and ride this out."

As the two vehicles pulled up to the old house, the original ranch house his grandfather had built, Hank laid on the wrap around porch which encircled the entire house underroof. Two paramedics were working on the elderly man in a flurry of excitement, as a few of the sheriff's deputies combed the area around the house with shot guns in hand.

Grady jumped from the vehicle and ran to the porch as the others slid out of Jed's vehicle. Jed immediately grabbed Valerie and held her back. "Let 'em have their space, Valerie."

"I'm a doctor, Jed. This is the kind of thing I deal with all day," shoving him away and rushing to the porch. She pulled the others back and looked over the struggling man, who laid on the porch bleeding, and began asking the paramedics questions. She started giving orders to the two men as she pulled his shirt off and looked up at the group. "It's pretty bad, Donny. Get Grady out of here! Take him to the fire. He doesn't need to see this."

Patsy picked up Hank Simmons' shot gun and immediately started unloading it. As Grady tried to go in the house, she grabbed him. "No … no, no Grady. You can't go in right now. Donavan, do as Dr. Dobbins said!"

He began walking in circles as he started to cry out, gabbing his hair. Jed and Donavan pulled him to the truck, forcing him into it. Betsy stayed to help Valerie. They jumped in the truck and the two began to pray with earnest for old Hank. They prayed for peace and God's intervention.

Jed started the truck and quickly headed out for the house in the center of the prairie. As they pulled up to the chaotic scene, he stopped the truck and they watched from a distance as the fire crew poured water on the remains of the house, a collapsed and smoldering pile of burning, black timbers. Jimmy pulled up behind them and stepped from his vehicle and walked solemnly to the truck. He opened the right side of the cab, watching Donavan and Grady get out and looked on them with tears in his own eyes. Grady sunk to the ground on his knees and watched as the scene played out in front of him.

The group stood for a half-hour of horror, watching the fire crews who looked on helplessly, unable to do anything but spray water till the flame was gone and a white smoke wafted from the pile of rubble. Officer Jernigan pulled up with Betsy in the car. "We need to get him to the hospital, Jimmy. The ambulance is on the way there now."

Donny and Jed slid in the truck as Jimmy loaded Grady in his command vehicle and transferred Betsy to his car, as well. "Sit with him, Betsy, and keep him calm." He walked over to Patsy and said, "What's done is done. You take over. I'm going with him to the hospital. The two of us helped his Daddy build this house. I need to be with Bill and Uncle Hank right now."

Grady sat in the back of the SUV and stared out the window. Betsy watched him with concern and compassion. She understood the things that made a man what he was. Grady had most of it stripped from him in less than two hours. She kept thinking through the study she and Jed were doing on the book of Job. How Job had lost everything in a matter of hours and lay sick in bed without even a comforting word from his wife. What an irony that was being played out in front of her right now.

As she looked at the beauty of the Sierra Mountains which rose high above the valley, trying to make sense of what was happening, Jimmy's cell phone rang. He clicked it on and said, "Darla, I need you to call Patsy. I put her in charge of the...." but he stopped abruptly and sat in silence as the dispatcher spoke. After a long pause, he stopped the command vehicle and got out, walking away from it as he carried the conversation on.

Darla said, "I just got a call from the Forest Service, Jimmy. There's a fire up at Red Mill Ranch. I didn't want to tell you over the radio. They're calling for us to get up there and take control of the scene. I went onto the shared response site to look at their dispatch log. It says multiple structure fires. What should I do?"

He looked away from the car as he wiped his eyes and said, "How many men are there from Temple Ridge?"

"They sent three men. I already called our guys in who had the day off. They're suiting up right now in the locker room. That gives us a total of six."

He paced back and forth, thinking this through. *"How much more destruction could happen?"*

"I need four of the cars on the street in Rails End and another car in Dr. Dobbin's driveway. Send Sam Cathay up to Red Mill Ranch. I want a Lieutenant up there. You tell the three boys from Temple Ridge and the other two from our office, if anything happens right now in Rails End, they arrest 'em and lock 'em up. Shot guns in the seat locks, not in the trunk, Darla. They need to be on the street patrolling, not drinking coffee someplace. When word gets out about all this, the town just might hold a lynching." Before he hung-up he ordered, "And call the plant and the Roadhouse and make sure Mac and my brother know about Uncle Hank."

When the vehicles arrived at the Meadows Regional Clinic, Jimmy pulled Jed and Donavan aside and gave them the news about the fires at Red Mill Ranch. "I think you two better get up there and give your staff some support. Right now, those boys are going through this without one of you there. I'll take care of Bill Simmons."

Jed, Betsy and Donavan packed into Jed's truck and sped off.

As Sheriff Jackson entered the emergency entrance, he looked back at the ambulance, which sat with the back doors open. *"What a mess! This isn't good,"* he thought, looking into the vehicle at the strewn and bloody bandages which lay on the floor.

Jimmy walked down the hall to the surgery room and sat down next to Grady, who was staring back at him with a look of panic. "They tried to burn Hank's house, Jimmy!" Grady stood up walking back and forth between the walls of the small hall, grabbing a chair and flinging it hard against the wall in despair.

"Bill, just sit back down and be calm! We don't need another scene like what took place at the Cougar after Celia died!" He walked him over to the bench seat, the very seat Grady had spent the night on after the accident almost two years earlier. He held his hands tightly to comfort him.

Grady looked up with tears in his eyes. "He heard them shooting the cattle. He saw some men outside his house and was waiting for them and started shooting at them. After they shot him, they ran off. Valerie has him stabilized. She's in there with him right now, helping Mansfield. It's a good thing she was with us out there. She said he wouldn't have survived the ambulance ride back. He's in pretty bad shape."

He looked at Grady as his own eyes filled with tears. "We're gonna clear this bunch out of the Meadows area, Bill. You have my word on that. You can't do this kind of thing without making a few mistakes."

He stood up and walked down the hall a ways, calling his dispatch desk. "I need you to call Patsy Jernigan and make sure we have two men stationed at old Hank's place for the next twenty-four hours, Darla. I need you to get a couple of the volunteers to spend the week out at his house, watching it. Hank's going to be here for a few days."

Burl Avery stood at the light table with the glossy, white proof of the special edition's front page he printed off the type set printer, complete with color photos of the destruction at the Simmons ranch in the Meadowlands. One side of the front page was a sideline story with a photo of Hank Simmons. **"Beloved Rancher Ambushed**." The bottom of the page below the fold was a story about the fires at Red Mill Ranch. **"Old Mill Town Burns**."

Mac eyed the full-page proof as the light shined through the glossy, white velum. He looked up at Burl and stated, "Its good, Burl! That looks really nice! Straight to the point on all three headlines."

"The press is already running, Mac. We'll have them in the racks by noon. As soon as Jimmy called me about Billy Simmons' house burning, I sent a photographer up to the Canyon. You were right. Real good photos of the men trying to put the fire out at the church as it was burning. Here's the other three pages."

Mac shook his head. "I was right about the ranch. I never expected them to burn his dad's house and shoot all the livestock."

He looked down at the light table as Burl spread them across it. The second page was full of photos of dead cattle and the smoldering timbers of the Simmons estate house on the Acreage. The third page was a collage of the two structures on fire on the ranch up in the canyon. One side of the Red Mill church was partially burning as the men on the ranch were hosing it down. Another photo was the old 1950s style Mack fire engine which belonged to the ranch, sitting near the new Type III fire truck the Forest Service uses, hoses strewn across the ground from both trucks.

As he looked at the pictures of the second building, a cabin house, he knew exactly which place it was. The entire building was fully involved with flames, as one side was crumbling in the raging fire. He stared at the photos of the building and shook his head. "There's going to be a lot of anger when Bill Simmons gets up to that ranch and sees what's in these photos. Do me a favor, Burl. Leave them alone at the hospital. It's best that Bill doesn't know about the fires up in the canyon till he gets through what's going on with his uncle. He's had enough heartache for the moment."

Mac slapped him on the back. "This special edition of yours is going to do for us what I've been trying to get done for years. It's time to sweep that group of cockroaches out of this town and the Meadowlands for good. They may think they're smart enough to pull all of this off in one day, but when the town sees just what they did ... well ... I learned a long time ago not to go up against public opinion when the whole town's angry." Mac just smiled and walked away. As he reached the door of the small building, he turned back and called out to Burl, "That half page ad on the back of the section that Bonner's Market is running. Does it have to be in the special edition, or can it run in tomorrow's paper?"

Burl looked surprised by the question. "No, he usually runs it in tomorrow's edition. But I already told him it was running in the special."

"Do me a personal favor. Stop your press and throw out what you've printed. I'll pay for the cost to re-plate the press and the paper expenses. Put a half page of news bites together in place of the ad and make sure the story about the Jenkins, Givers and Brines all being related is in with the mix. Nothing big or flashy. Just make it look like it was part of the stories you put in to fill the space. Tell Rick over at the market you couldn't put the ad in and give it to him free tomorrow. Go ahead and put the charge for the ad onto my account for the harvest festival printing you're doing for the plant."

Burl laughed with a shake of his head. "You should have been a newsman! That's how it's done! Slip it out there nice and subtle like, after the three pages of destruction they caused. A dandy of an idea, Mac!"

- 14 -

JOB'S REMORSE

Valerie walked out into the hall and sat on a bench while Grady had time with his uncle in private. He was stable as he lay in the bed of the ICU, talking in a weak voice with his nephew and sons. Thirty minutes later, Grady came out in the hallway and sat with her.

She had spent the half-hour sitting in her surgeon's scrubs, with her back against the hard, light green wall of the hallway, while she rested with her eyes closed. She slid over tight against her fiancé and took his arm into hers. The tension of the morning had subsided, and the sorrow of the day's events overwhelmed her. She buried her face into his shoulder and began to cry. "How does so much evil exist in a family?"

Grady turned and put his arms around her, pulling her back to his chest and just held her tight, crying with her. Dr. Mansfield looked around the corner of the receptionist desk as her voice carried loudly down the hall with an echo, listening to the wail of her crying. He had never seen the rigid woman like this before. She was normally so in control in his clinic. In fact, at times, he wondered if she had any emotions at all when she was performing her job.

The older doctor came over to the couple and sat with them. "Valerie, why don't you take the rest of the week off? I think you need to be with Bill right now. We can get by for a few days without you." He stood up and walked the couple to the glass doors of the lobby. "I'll take care of Hank. Don't worry about him, Bill. He's doing fine. You need to get up to the canyon and take care of the mess that happened up there this morning."

Grady looked up with concern. "What are you talking about, Doc? We came from my Daddy's ranch this morning."

Dr. Mansfield lifted his head with a deep breath and walked to the news rack outside the door, putting two quarters in it and pulling a paper from the stack. He handed it to the couple with a grave look, "I'm sorry, Bill. I thought you knew about the ranch," turning the folded paper over to show him the bottom of the page.

As they stared at the page, Grady exploded in anger.

Valerie yelled, **"Burning the ranch makes no sense! Why would they do that? They have nothing to gain from it!"**

Grady fumed as he looked at the two doctors. "They don't care about the buildings! They're going to level the place and build houses. They did it to make it personal. That raging inferno right there is Jed and Betsy's house! The other one is the church!"

She shrank back with a look of horror as she held her hand to her mouth. She almost collapsed as she began crying again. Mansfield said, "Wait here." He went inside and called Brittany, the receptionist, to the door. "Take Dr. Dobbins and Mr. Simmons up to Red Mill. I'll get someone to cover the counter."

The three of them drove into the ranch as Valerie continued to softly cry, leaning against Grady in the back seat of the car. Brittany slowly drove past the pavilion and approached the group who stood in the middle of the road. She gasped, "Oh my gosh!" Nothing but a pile of black timbers and blowing ash lay around the rock foundation of the Gentry's cabin. Nothing was left but the fireplace and a rock structure which was once the kitchen stove. The small, black potbellied stove that had sat on the corner of the porch was laying on its side, still attached to the crumpled stovepipe. It was the only evidence of what had once been the evening gathering place which had provided so many years of pleasure for the entire ranch staff.

Jed helped Betsy to her feet where the woman had knelt in a crumpled manner and Valerie ran to her, hugging her as they cried together.

"Thirty years, Grady," he said. "Thirty years and it's all gone! Everything we owned was in that house. And that doesn't even begin to account for the pain of the memories. I raised both of my kids in this house." Jed pulled a hanky from his pocket and blew his nose, looking up at him with red eyes.

After a long silence, he said, "When we were watching that house of your Daddy's burn this morning, all I could think of was how you and Donny had suffered so badly. I almost felt guilty. Then I got back here and watched the smoldering beams burn. It had already collapsed when we arrived. The only things we have left are the clothes we're wearing and the truck."

Jonathon and Jason approached the two men. "I'm sorry, Grady. When we arrived up here to the ranch in the Polaris, the buildings were already burning. We had to make a choice. Put the fire out at Jed's cabin or put out the fire at the church. The Forest Service wasn't here yet."

He looked at the two, young men, putting a hand on Jason's shoulder. "You made the right choice. The church is in the center of the village. You stopped the whole place from going up."

Jason looked up with a sad reflection. "Actually, that's not why we chose the church. Honestly, we weren't even thinking about the town."

He turned his head to the side with a look out of one eye. "Why did you choose to put out the church fire then?"

"We just asked each other WWJD! What would Jed do? He would have told us to save the church and let his house burn. That's just what we did!"

Jed looked up at him with tears in his eyes and started laughing. "He's right, Cowboy. That's exactly what I would have done!" He gave the men a hug and said, "You did well, boys. You did the right thing! We can rebuild the cabin house. But the church? The history of that place goes back to the thirties. It was the first church ever built up in this part of the Sierras. It was here before a single building went up in Rails End. The original house of God still stands. Yep ... you did the right thing!"

After a few minutes, he looked up at the men with a hearty smile. "Thank you for that! I needed to hear that right about now. It makes it a lot easier knowing this old cabin had to burn in order to save the church. And you saved the village, as well."

Grady looked down and kicked some dirt with the front of his boot. "It really don't matter. We can't back the bid now that the estate house on the Acreage is destroyed and the herd is dead. In a few days the Jenkins and the Givers are gonna come in here with a bunch of bull dozers and level the place. I can promise you that." As he looked on at the group of mourners, he called out, "Let's go to the hall everyone. It's time for a prayer meeting. We got nothing left. Everything Jed, Donny and I own is gone. We're gonna get on our knees and put this in God's hands. He's the only thing I have left, other than Valerie and my daughters."

He looked at the older man with a long sigh of resignation. "Psalms 22, Jed! I'm gonna get that Bible Val gave me. It's up at my cabin. I'll meet you in the meeting hall. When we get there, I want you to read it to everyone."

When the staff was assembled in the meeting hall, Jed opened the leather-bound Bible and flipped to the Old Testament. He began to read the same Scripture he read to Grady, Valerie and Betsy that night, the previous year, when they had been attacked by Peggy Withers in this same meeting hall.

"But I am a worm and not a man, scorned by everyone, despised by the people. All who see me mock me; they hurl insults, shaking their heads. "He trusts in the LORD," they say, "let the LORD rescue him. Let him deliver him, since he delights in him." Yet you brought me out of the womb; you made me trust

in you, even at my mother's breast. From birth I was cast on you; from my mother's womb you have been my God. Do not be far from me, for trouble is near and there is no one to help". -Psalms 22:6-11

He skipped down to verse 19 and read:

"But you, LORD, do not be far from me. You are my strength; come quickly to help me. Deliver me from the sword, my precious life from the power of the dogs. Rescue me from the mouth of the lions; save me from the horns of the wild oxen. I will declare your name to my people; in the assembly I will praise you. You who fear the LORD, praise him! All you descendants of Jacob, honor him! Revere him, all you descendants of Israel! For he has not despised or scorned the suffering of the afflicted one; he has not hidden his face from him but has listened to his cry for help." -Psalms 22:19-24

Jed called the group to prayer and they all knelt in a circle in the room, prostrating themselves down to the wooden floor. One-by-one, they began to pray.

After ten minutes, Valerie looked up with one eye open. She watched as Jonathon silently exited the hall to head down to the Rails End bus stop to pick up Crissy and her sisters. And as much as she wanted to see the girls, she knew a storm was coming. Her silent prayer turned from mourning for what had taken place that day, to a pleading to God for his peace over this man who she knelt next to.

As Jed had said to Grady just a few weeks before, their coming in the middle of what was taking place was bad timing. The girl should have come clean with her father long before now. She feared for both Crissy and Jonathon. Grady had already been stretched to his breaking point, and beyond.

- 15 -

A PERFECT STORM

Mac stood in the third-floor office of the rail yard plant. He looked across the yard of ore cars and engines at the crowd who had gathered on the steps of town hall in the downtown area. As he watched the agitated group of a hundred people, Rick Seavey walked up with two cups of coffee, handing one to Mac. They both looked out the window as Rick shook his head. "I sure hope you know what you're doing, Mac. Personally, I think this whole plan of yours is a shake of the dice."

Mac just looked on for a minute and then turned toward the leather, sofa chairs in his office, inviting him over to sit and talk. "I called you to pray with me each day during the last two weeks because I needed a prayer partner on this. The whole idea came to me in a dream. And it wasn't without wise counsel. Jim Jackson, Burl and I talked that dream out. After a lot of thought, we decided it had merit. I asked you into this because I'm not stupid. If it was of the Lord, I wanted a man beside me who could give good, spiritual counsel." He looked Rick in the eyes and said, "Do you know why I started going back to church?"

He shook his head and breathed in hard. "No, Mac, I don't. But I've wondered about why you suddenly came to your senses and got your life straight with the Lord?"

"Almost two years ago, after Bill Simmons had that accident, I saw the two of you in his office and you were praying with him. Bill had gone through a tough time after Celia's death. Everyone in the office could see what was going on. The man refused to take some time off. I offered him a six-month, paid leave to put his family back together. But it wasn't until you spoke with him that day that he actually started to deal with the issues. And to be completely honest, I watched Bill come back to life."

He took a sip from his coffee cup and continued. "I have to tell you, Rick, we all tried to give him advice, but the advice you gave him was to start with the Lord. You know, running this place was something I wasn't prepared for when it happened. I took the old man for granted. I thought he was always going to be there and in charge. When the ownership was passed to me ... well ... I just sort of got so busy with managing I let go of the Lord in my life. The money I was making as the owner didn't help any. It was a slow process, but it happened, nonetheless. I wasn't happy, Rick. I know that sounds sort of dumb, but I wasn't. I let the power and money destroy my life. Then my wife wanted a divorce."

"No Mac, it doesn't sound dumb. It's a common mistake. Things don't make up for God in a man's life. Riches, success, it's all fleeting. In the end, when we pass on, we're all accountable as we stand before the Lord and the one question He's going to ask is, *What did you do with your life? How many souls did you help to bring to the Lord?*"

Mac gave him an honest and humble look. "I saw such a dramatic change in Bill after that day that it shamed me. I suddenly realized what I had done. And from that day forward, I loaded the family back in the car on Sunday mornings and got my heart right with God. And in a way, *you* were responsible for that. So, when this whole thing started heating up and those dark clouds began to swirl over Rails End, I knew I needed to call you to pray through this with me."

He put his coffee cup down. "Rick, it all happened, just like in the dream. Those spiritual clouds of darkness I saw in the dream were coming true. I could see it. Jimmy could see it. Even Burl could see it. The dream stopped short of what took place today, but I knew God was calling me to be the one to prepare for it. God still uses prophecy today. I know those of us who grew up in the reformed tradition don't always see it. But in my book, every time the Lord uses a man to give the pastor wisdom about a building project, or a deacon knows just what to do when an issue arises which leaves everyone else stumped, it's the voice of God whispering in his ear. That's prophetic, Rick! And when God gives a man a dream as clear as the one he gave me, the man needs to think real hard about where that dream came from."

He stood up and walked to the window, watching the crowd down in the town. "I've been here long enough to know the people of Rails End can be trusted to do the right thing. But sometimes they need a little push." He looked back at Rick and said, "When the images from those cameras we put on the ranch last night come back, we'll know just how truthful the dream was. And I have you to thank for that suggestion. It came out of our prayer time together. It wasn't Bill who told me about those families being related. The Lord showed it to me in the dream. The Lord will clean them out of this town for good. And if you ask me, they sure did pick on the wrong guy. The Simmons family has done as much as mine to build this town, and every one of those people down there know it!"

Jonathon and Crissy sat in a booth by the windows at the Roadhouse Restaurant with Missy and Shawny. The four of them watched the crowd of people gathered across the street as the young man recounted the past two months to them: The news about his giving his life to Christ, the bids for ownership of Red Mill Canyon and the events of the day. The girls were in tears as he told them the news about their great-uncle, Hank, being shot. Shawny and Missy wanted to go to the hospital, but Crissy remained silent and tearful. "I don't know how to tell Daddy I'm pregnant, Johnny. He's gonna know as soon as he sees me. Someone needs to talk to him first."

All three sets of eyes were on Jonathon as they waited for an answer. "Oh Man! ... Okay, I'm gonna have to be the one to do it, but one of you needs to be there with me." He looked at Missy and Shawny. Shawny felt it was his responsibility and didn't want to be in the room when her dad found out, but she had empathy for him. "We better get going. It'll be dark in an hour."

As the four stood up to leave, they watched Jeremy Traeger enter the restaurant, handing out fliers to everyone sitting in the Roadhouse eating. As they looked at the flier, it read in bold letters:

"Don't Do Business With A Family
Who Burns Down Your Neighbor's House!
We Don't Need The Jenkins, The Givers
And The Brines In This Town!"

Photocopied on the bottom of the flier was the story from the back page of the special edition about the families being related.

Jonathon looked up at the three girls. "Let's get out of here before things really start to heat up. I don't want to be around when this gets out of hand, even if they *do* have it coming!"

Valerie, Jed and Betsy sat pensively in Grady's cabin as Jonathon's truck pulled up to the house. Jonathon and Shawny opened the screen door to the small cabin house and Valerie gave the girl a big hug. Grady came into the room, looking haggard, and stared out of the window. "Where's Missy and Crissy? I thought all three of you were coming?"

"They're … umm … they're talking to Jason right now."

When the awkwardness of the moment became obvious, Valerie was the first to speak. "Grady, you need to come to the table and sit down. Jonathon needs to talk to you first before you see the girls."

He took a seat next to Valerie, and Shawny sat on the other side, next to her father. Jonathon sat across the table, staring at the floor. He looked up to speak but didn't know what to say. He had rehearsed this moment many times in his head, but now his mind was a blank. "Grady, sir ... ummm ..." *and his voice trailed off to nothing.* He felt suddenly sick to his stomach.

Valerie loudly cleared her throat and stared across the table at the young man who was trying to avoid eye contact with anyone. Jed and Betsy sat on the couch and silently prayed through the moment. Jed looked up at Jonathon. "Get on with it, boy. Don't just leave the man sitting there!"

Jonathon looked up a little braver after Jed's demand. "Grady, Crissy's gonna have a baby!" As he tried to say more, his eyes began to fill with tears, and he looked down again.

Valerie put her arm to his back as Shawny turned to look at her father. And after a long silence, she put her hand on his arm. "Daddy, do you understand what Jonathon is saying? Crissy's pregnant." Jonathon suddenly stood and headed for the door. And then he was gone.

Grady sat on his chair with a feeling of overwhelming pain and betrayal. He looked at the others with bewilderment, and then at Valerie. "You knew about this?"

She knew he would ask her this question, eventually. She wasn't expecting him to connect the dots so quickly. "Crissy came to me to be tested. She needed to know for sure. Yes, Grady, I've known about it for a few months now. But it wasn't my place to tell you. She needed to be the one to do it."

He looked around the room. "You all knew about this or you wouldn't be here right now!" He got up from the table and slowly walked outside to the end of the porch. He looked out at the meadow. And in that moment, the weight of the entire day came crashing down on him as he sobbed on the porch. It had all been taken from him. Everything was gone. Even the trust and loyalty of his daughter and those around him were gone. Valerie, Jed, Betsy, Jonathon; they all knew, and no one said a word. While he stood on the porch, the others sat in silence in the cabin.

After a long spell on the porch, he composed himself. He looked out on the meadow and the anger started to build. The father of three went back into the cabin and stood there with his hands on his hips. "I can't even trust the college to look after my daughter!" He stared at Shawny with fire in his eyes. Jed had seen this look many times before. "I want to know who the boy is and why he isn't here with you right now!"

Shawny looked up in amazement as Valerie and Jed shot a glance at each other. They suddenly realized he didn't understand. Jed and Valerie both stood in a panic and Shawny looked down knowing she wasn't the one to speak. She had no clue what to say.

As the two walked toward him, he became indignant with Shawny. **"Who is he, girl? I want to know!"**

Valerie said with a trembling voice, "Grady, come over here and sit for a moment." Jed tried to put his hand on his shoulder, but his friend shoved his arm off and stared Shawny down, as she looked up in horror. He was a volcano that was ready to blow. She had seen her father this way many times before.

Betsy stood and faced him. "It's Jonathon. They've been dating since Christmas. Now sit down at the table and let's talk this out."

That was news he couldn't bear. He stood with his mouth open, and his mind reeled as he thought through the months like a calendar that was spinning. Grady whipped around and headed for the door at a quick pace. Jed tried to block him, only to be knocked to the floor. Valerie jumped from her seat to follow but he turned and walked back through the room, pushing her aside as he stepped to the fireplace. He jerked the rifle from the gun rack and shoved the group back.

Shawny began to plead with him. Valerie yell at him, trying to grab him. "Grady, no! You can't do this! Grady! ... **Grady!**"

He stormed from the cabin, walking with a quicker pace from the porch and across the lawn, turning to the path which led in front of the cabins. Valerie ran to the field phone in the kitchen and cranked the dial four times. She kept repeating the motion, over and over, till Donavan picked up the phone in the maintenance shop. "Donny, Grady's headed your way with his gun. He just found out Jonathon's the one who got Crissy pregnant. You need to stop him,

Donny!"

He darted out the door and across the road to the bunkhouse. He threw the door open, looking at Jason, Jonathon, Missy and Crissy. "Jason, get out here! The rest of you lock the door. Grady's headed this way." As Jonathon slammed the door behind them and locked it, Crissy hugged him and began to cry.

The two men started running and rounded the corner of the maintenance shed, heading up Staff Row to meet him. Donavan put his hands out and yelled at him. **"You can't do this, Grady!"** He tried to march past them and the two began to tussle with him, fighting over the gun. As they struggled, both men grabbed his arms, forcing him back. **"Grady ... Grady! Just stop for a minute!"**

He flipped the field rifle and snapped it back, pointing it at the two with the gun to his shoulder. "I'll use it on you first if you don't get out of my way, Donny!"

Donavan stepped back with his hands on his hips and said, "No you won't. The gun isn't loaded. There's no bullets in it." As he stood there with the rifle to his shoulder at a standoff, Valerie and Jed caught up with him and started pleading.

He repeated his words. "The gun's empty, Grady. Just put it down. I unloaded it as soon as I got up to the ranch today. I knew you might try to use it after everything that happened this morning. It was just a matter of time before you grabbed it. They pushed you too far. They pushed all of us too far. I went through your cabin and your office and unloaded the 30/30 and the shot gun. And I took every bullet I could find."

After a long pause he said, "I unloaded all of the guns on the ranch. I went through every building. And no one's getting their bullets back until this entire mess is over."

Grady lowered the rifle and unlatched it, looking in the chamber. It was empty, just like he said.

Jed gently took the rifle from him and handed it to Donavan. "Killing the boy won't resolve the issue. You stand at a crossroads right now. One direction is filled with pain. You'll never see your daughter again if you take it. Do you really think Val will marry you after killing your grandchild's father? And you'll never be able to hold your grandchild. You'll live with the fact you killed the baby's father, for the rest of your life."

"The other road is a road of love, Grady. A wedding to the woman you love. A grandbaby to hold and your family surrounding you for the rest of your life. Which road are ya' gonna take, Cowboy? The road of misery and pain, or the road you talked about the other night, a chance to start over?"

Betsy said, "Grady, for some reason God chose to do to us what he did to Job. He allowed Satan to take all we have today. But He left you your family. In fact, He's giving you a grandchild. Job lost his whole family. And the Bible makes it clear when you read the book of Job, it's God who allowed Satan to take it from him. The whole conversation started at the throne of God. In fact, it was God who brought Job's name up in the first place! Do you know why he did it? To prove to Satan a righteous man who serves Him is stronger than Satan himself." She leaned forward and said, "That's you, Grady! It's a perfect description of you!" Betsy hugged him and started crying.

The group of friends surrounded him and began to pray. He fell to his knees and cried out to God asking him why. "Why would God allow this day of evil to happen?"

- 16 -

REFINER'S FIRE

But that day belongs to the Lord, the Lord Almighty—
a day of vengeance, for vengeance on his foes… (Jer. 46:10a)

Sheriff Jackson woke to his home phone loudly ringing the following morning. He could hear his wife in the other room as she spoke. "Okay, Darla. I'll wake him up. He's still in bed." No sooner did she hang up when the phone rang again.

He quickly dressed as Beatrice talked on the phone. He came out to a wife who had concern written all over her face. "I think you better get to the office, Jimmy. They're getting some calls."

He jumped in his vehicle and called the Dispatch number. Darla informed the sheriff she had seven calls already about graffiti and broken windows. Three of the locations were owned by the Givers Development Company and a few had come in about the Jenkin's bar and grill out at the edge of town.

As he drove by the Givers' office downtown, the plate glass windows were shattered, glass scattering the sidewalk. Another unit was already there, and the officer had stepped through the window to survey the damage. "I don't have a problem if you want me to just drive off right now, Jimmy, and leave the mess for them to figure out."

He pretended not to hear the snide comment, "Make a call to the Givers house. Let 'em know what happened."

"I already did. No one's answering. This is the third location I've been to that they own. Thank God they didn't torch the place.

The sign at the entrance of their new housing development, over on the south side, has been torn down and broken into pieces. And their truck yard where they park their equipment was vandalized. Every windshield is smashed, and the trucks and bulldozers are all full of graffiti."

Jimmy said, "I don't think they counted on everyone finding out about their being related to the Brines and the Jenkins families." He stood there, grinding his teeth as he looked at the mess. He turned to the other officer and quoted a verse from the book of Revelation. *"I looked, and there before me was a pale horse! Its rider was named Death, and Hades was following close behind him." -Revelation 6:8a*

The officer looked at him quizzically and the Sheriff ordered, "Radio Darla and tell her I said to call the men in again who are off duty. It's going to be a long day."

He drove out to the highway beyond Main Street to the Towns End Bar and Grill the Jenkins family owned. Sure enough, the windows had been busted out and mounds of trash and garbage had been tossed at the front of the building, blocking the entrance. He slid out and surveyed the inside of the bar with his flashlight as he stepped over the bags of rotting trash which covered the sidewalk. *"Well, at least the trash everyone was dumping was a fitting statement,"* he mused. He watched as a few cars slowly drove by, and then sped away.

Valerie stood on the porch of Grady's cabin with the comforter from his bed wrapped around her. Her fiancé had fallen asleep on the couch early in the evening and had slept all night. She decided she better not leave, so she had fallen asleep on the big comforter in his bedroom. Grady was now sitting on one of the boulders which dotted the landscape, arms on his knees and his head bowed. She watched him with a look of concern before going back inside to get breakfast started for everyone.

In the middle of cooking breakfast, she walked to the screen door to find Donavan approaching Grady. Jonathon was with him. Tears welled up in her eyes and she sat in his big, sofa chair and started fervently praying. *"Lord, please ... please make him listen. Show him how to have mercy, Lord. Give Grady a heart of forgiveness."*

She heard the sound of boots on the porch as the three men took a seat. After a long silence, Jonathon mustered the courage to speak. "I'm sorry, Grady. I really am. I never intended to hurt you. If I had it all to do over again in the last few months, it never would've happened. We ... we just got carried away. It happened during Springtide."

As he stared off in the distance, not wanting to look the boy in the face, Donavan moved closer to him, sitting on the swinging love seat next to him. "Grady, there's a handful of things I wish I could change about my life before I came to the Lord. What he did was wrong, but it wasn't anything worse than some of the dumb stuff I did. He's a brother in the Lord now. Hear him out."

He looked up and asked, "What's your plan, Jonathon? You can talk till the sun goes down, but what I want to know is, what are your intentions from here on out with my daughter?"

"I love her. We've had two months to talk this out. I want to marry Crissy."

Donavan shot him a glance of disapproval and he corrected his statement. "Grady ... I'm ... I'm asking for your daughter's hand in marriage. I totally understand if you don't approve of it. And if you tell me to, I'll pack my stuff and get off the ranch before the day is over. But I want you to know I want to marry her. And I'm promising I'll raise the child in a godly household."

Valerie prayed harder now as she listened to the silence coming from the porch. And then he spoke. "What's done is done, Johnny. It can't be undone." He contemplated the moment as he looked out at the meadow. "Okay, I'll agree to this. But it's gonna be done right. This week you start counseling with Reverend Spicer. You need to be married before the baby's born. And I don't want to hear another word about it once you *are* married. Every kid deserves to know he's a gift from God, not some product of a *romp* in the hay. I want to hear from Crissy this is what she wants."

After the two men left, she came out and sat next to him, wiping the tears from her eyes. She took one of his big hands into her own, holding it in a comforting manner. "Thank you, Bill. Give it time. Time heals the wounds." She leaned back against the swing seat and slid over against him. "We haven't lost everything. We still have my house and vehicles. And I guess it's time to start using that truck you bought me. The thing has sat in my driveway since the winter snow cleared."

He put his arm around her as she laid her head to his shoulder. While they rocked, she said, "Actually this child just might be a blessing in disguise. I've struggled with the thought that if we have children of our own, you'd be seventy when the first child leaves for college. I can't say that I've ever been busy thinking about having children of my own. It's bad enough being a doctor and trying to carry on a normal life on some days. Maybe God's giving you a grandchild to bring up and teach, the way your grandfather taught you."

He looked down at her and smiled weakly. "Maybe, Val." And then he admitted, "I never would have expected this from Crissy. She was always the good one. She always did the right thing." He wiped the tears from his face.

No sooner had breakfast ended than a scattered arrival of cars began to fill the ranch. Jed stared out of the window with a sad look. "Sorry to say, boss, but I think it's gonna be a busy day. That Mercedes out there is Dougy Thomas' car. I see Frank Jones with him. I'm sure he's here to survey the damage and talk insurance. I guess we might as well go out and discuss the bad news with him."

After a long hesitation, he said, "I'm sorry, Grady. I was really looking forward to running this place and making it into something with you. I guess it's time to call my kids and let them know what's going on. But first, we need to speak to Doug."

The four men walked the ranch, looking at the remains of Jed's cabin and checking the damage to the church building. Doug looked at the mess and shook his head. "It isn't right. No one should be allowed to do what that family did and then get the bid. But until there's proof of any wrongdoing on the part of Jack Jenkins, there's nothing I can do. If you can't back your bid, he gets the property. I have to follow the laws."

Mac Grady, and Rick Seavey stepped from another car and approached the group of men. Rick walked up and gave him a hug. Mac looked around at the damage and just grimaced without a word. Mac had two forms of communication, being the most demanding voice in a room or being silent. Today he was silent. Grady knew he wasn't happy, and it could be unnerving to watch him, wondering what was really going on in his head.

After a few minutes, Rick Maretti and Mac were surveying the damage to the church. A half-hour later they were down at the cow pasture going through the rubble of Jed and Betsy's cabin. Grady didn't give it another thought. Mac was always about detail, no matter what he was doing. And both men were part of the Owners Association.

After some discussion, Doug announced a second bid meeting to all the men in attendance. "The board will be up tonight. Have the staff present, Bill. I had a call first thing this morning from Jack Jenkins demanding a rebid meeting. The second call I received was from his lawyer. I'm sorry, Bill, but we need to get this thing done and move on." He darted his eyes from Grady, to Mac, and over to Rick and quickly looked away so the crowd standing around them didn't notice. Valerie stared at Doug and glanced at Grady with a furrow to her brow, noticing the sudden exchange of eyes.

Rick took Grady back to his cabin and they sat on the porch to talk about the events of the previous day. "You know, the town's pretty upset right now. All of the Givers' businesses were really trashed during the night. And the Jenkins' suffered the same fate."

He pulled his phone from his pocket and held it up to show Grady the picture of the piles of trash on the porch of the bar and grill, which was now a mountain of bags and broken pieces of furniture four feet high which spanned the length of the entire front of the building. "I guess the folks down in Rails End have had enough of their ilk." Grady smiled weakly and looked off at the onlookers who walked around the ranch.

"Sheriff Jackson has kept it under control. In fact, the town's pretty silent right now. Every cop car from Rails End and Temple Ridge are cruising the streets in town." Grady wanted to take the higher road here, but it just wasn't in him. He simply remained silent. Rick said, "I hope this plan of yours works tonight."

Grady quickly looked around and shook his head. "Don't talk about it! Just let the meeting tonight play out."

Valerie walked out on the porch wearing an apron and put her arm around their future best man. "I want you to stay for dinner, Rick. It's probably going to be our last up here. Jed already has the smoker running down at the pavilion. After the meeting we're going to throw caution to the wind and have a big to-do. We all agreed having a big barbeque was the only fitting way to give everyone a chance to share their stories. And to be honest, it's giving Jed something to do to stay busy. Betsy and I gathered all the baking supplies from the other ladies. We're all inside doing some baking."

At four-thirty, so many cars had entered the front gate of Red Mill Ranch that Owen was on his radio calling for help. Jonathon and Donavan were giving out orders to the staff as they turned every possible spot into parking and tried to keep order in the midst of all the chaos.

At five o'clock, the hall was packed. Jed looked around at all the people. "Now there's a sight you don't often see!" he laughed. "Cowboys sitting next to people wearing suits. I think half the town's here as well as most of the owners."

Jack Jenkins stood from the group who he was sitting with, not even trying to hide his affiliation with his family any longer. Jared Brine and his brothers sat with Ron Givers and the rest of Ron's family.

Donavan leaned forward to Grady, who was sitting in front of him and stated, "They have a lot of gall being in this room tonight."

He quietly said, "After what Rick told me today, I'm sure they're sticking together tight to protect themselves. I see they brought their lawyer with them."

As Doug was about to call the meeting to order, Sheriff Jackson walked into the room with a few deputies and they stood at the back of the hall with their arms crossed, looking out at the packed room. Mac stood up and walked to the sheriff, chatting quietly with him for a few seconds before walking back to his chair. Sheriff Jackson's brother, Johnny, walked through the door with his oldest son, Junior, and gave him a solid stare. "Is everything ready?"

Jimmy nodded. "Yep! It ends right here in this hall tonight."

"Good! Sheriff Wilkins should have ended it forty-five years ago, but he didn't have the backbone to do it." Johnny and his son walked down the back of the room and took a seat with Mac.

Mac said, "You made it."

He drew in a deep breath, "This fight has been slowly brewing for forty-five years between us and the Givers, ever since they shot Uncle Hank the first time. It's time to end it! We took an oath forty years ago to protect the welfare of our town. That's why our names are carved on that tree up on the hill." As he settled in and his eyes scanned the room, he leaned toward Mac and said, "How many lawyers did you and Billy dig up? There has to be about a dozen of them in the room right now."

Doug regained control of the meeting as the room fell silent, and pulled the bid envelope open again. "Before I proceed with this process, I have a question for Bill Simmons, Jed Gentry and Donavan Rice. Bill, we set a date to the bid process, which is registered with the state due to the laws regarding the sale of land that's fully bordered by Forest Service land. We have to stick to that date. We have no say in the matter."

The echo of boos filled the hall from the crowd, and Doug waited till they were quiet. "If it were up to me ... and I'm sure the board agrees with me on this ... I would extend the time on this, but I can't. Bill, do you have the means to back the bid?"

Grady stood, walking to the front of the room. "Doug, the estate house was insured. But it's gonna take some time for that to get all settled out. The cattle operation..." and then he became silent for a moment as he looked down on the floor. "We weren't insured for some bunch of lowlifes coming onto the ranch and shooting every cow on the place." He looked toward the crooked gathering of relatives where the Brines, Jenkins and Givers were seated and just stared them down. "The insurance company won't cover that. I had a meeting about it with the Jones Agency this afternoon."

Jared elbowed his brother Joey and they stared back at Grady with a smile. Jack stood and yelled, **"Get on with it, Doug, or I'll have my lawyer serve you with papers right here and now! He's ready for any waffling if you want it to go that way!"**

He breathed in deep and sighed. "Jack, I read the Ledger yesterday. It said you're related to the Brine and Givers families. Is that true?"

Jack's lawyer stood and tried to pull the man back to talk to him, but he brushed him off. "So, what if we are? I'm buying this place, not the Givers. There's no law against being related to someone. Get on with it!"

Doug stood his ground and said, "So you *are* related to the Brines and the Givers, as wells as Peggy Withers? I just want to get the point clear here. Or is the article from the newspaper wrong?"

When his lawyer heard Peggy's name, he yelled, **"Jack!"**

He looked back at the group behind him and turned back to Doug. "I said we were! Now get on with it!" The lawyer rolled his eyes and threw his palms in the air with an exasperated look, crossing his arms and turning his head, staring out the window next to his seat. Jennifer Thomas, Doug's sister, was sitting high with her back straight in the seat, watching Jack's lawyer as she looked down the row of people. She sat back with a smile and lifted her briefcase, pulling a thick, legal sized envelope from it. She handed it to one of the lawyers sitting next to her.

Johnny turned to look at his brother Jimmy, who was smiling his way. He turned the other way toward Mac and said, "Go give them the bad news." Mac reached for his own briefcase.

Doug straightened up from the podium he was leaning on and asked, "Mr. Simmons, at this point I need to let you know the original bid's still yours if you have a way to back the offer. I need to know now, if you do. But first I'm going to open the floor for public comment, which is my legal right to do as chairman of this proceeding."

Mac stood and walked forward. "I would like to make a statement if I may?" Doug swept his hand in a wide gesture toward the podium as he stood aside with a big grin on his face.

"My name's Mac Grady. I'm the owner and chairman of the Grady Corporation." He opened the envelope he was holding and held up a large contract. "I hold in my hand a contract which was signed by every member of my board yesterday. It states, in detail, an offer to Bill Simmons for rights to use the Simmons Ranch for a rail line which will provide for the expansion of the Grady Corporation's rails through the Meadowlands area. This expansion will allow for the additional rail cars to back up the new Harville mining operation in Furline Canyon. Harville signed the deal for the rights to the canyon with the Forest Service and the BLM yesterday. It already had approval."

He looked at Grady. "I also took the time to visit with each of your relatives yesterday afternoon, Bill. I have signed letters from every member of your family stating they're in favor of this agreement just in case someone wanted to hold up the proceedings with some kind of legal maneuvering. I know Stan Beasley is legal counsel for you in the matters relating to your ranch property. He's here if you would like to talk with him first. But I can tell you if you do accept it, I'm prepared to pay you two million over the course of the contract. And that's just for the rights during the next five years. If we extend it, which there's an option in the contract to do that, it's worth much … much … more. I have a check for one million as down payment on this agreement, right here."

Mac lifted a check from the envelope and held it up, showing it to the audience.

Valerie sat there with a stunned look on face. Stan Beasley stood. "Bill, the contract's good. I already reviewed it. I also had it reviewed by a lawyer who handles rail issues, who's acting as a consultant for me. It's a solid contract. I would say do it and let's get these proceedings over with."

Jack Jenkins grabbed his lawyer's coat with a fist full of material, talking in a heated exchange with him. The lawyer shook his head in exasperation. "You're an idiot, Jack. I tried to tell you to just shut up and don't say anything about your family. You just uncorked a firestorm because you wouldn't listen to me. This is nothing compared to what's coming next! I wash my hands of this whole mess. I'm not a trial lawyer. Get yourself another lawyer. I've already finished what I came here to do." The man stood and walked out of the room.

As all eyes followed the departing lawyer, Stan walked over to the tall cowboy and quietly said, "Come on my friend. It's time to flush this bunch of cockroaches out of this entire region." He stood and took Valerie's hand, pulling her up from her seat, and the three walked to the front as he stood there, looking at Mac. "I accept the offer!" The packed room of onlookers stood and cheered.

Mac pulled a pen from his pocket and said in a loud voice, "Bill Simmons, I want to bless you right now with a little present. It's the pen you signed the agreement for the bid with. I believe it was a gift from you, Doctor Dobbins, and from that young lady sitting over there with Jed Gentry." He read the inscription, "For Grandfather! Rick Maretti and I found it in the rubble of the Gentry's cabin today. I took it back to the office with me and had one of my men clean it up and replace the insides. The luster isn't so bright, but … well … I guess that just makes it all the more memorable after all this pen's been through in the last few days!"

Mac handed the pen to him, and the entire hall was fighting off tears. Stan flipped through the contract and showed him where to sign and on what pages. He then signed it as a witness. "Congratulations, Bill! Doug, my client's prepared to proceed with his bid. Can we move on with it now? I do believe this check and the contract is legal tender to back up the offer Mr. Simmons, Gentry and Rice are making. After all, Jack Jenkins over there wants to get this over with. I believe he made that very clear a few minutes ago!"

Doug took the check and asked the crowd to take a seat.

"Sheriff Jackson, can you come forward? You told me earlier you needed to talk with this crowd." Jackson walked to the podium and started to speak but looked down and quietly laughed. Then he apologized. "I sure hope I don't have to stand up here in the future, Bill Simmons, and make any more speeches. This is getting old, really fast."

He motioned to his deputies, who moved across the hall toward the stunned looking group who sat with Jack. "Jared and Joey Brine, the Rails End Sheriff's office is arresting you for arson. One of the owners of the Association installed cameras two days ago on the ranch. I have both of you on video lighting the fires that burned down the Gentry cabin and damaged the church building yesterday morning while the ranch staff was down the highway."

As the room quieted down, watching the two deputies handcuff the men, Jackson said, "Get 'em out of here, boys!" After the men were escorted out the door to the jeering crowd, Jackson continued. "Now, I'm sorry to say we still don't have immediately conclusive evidence of who attacked Hank Simmons, burned down his brother's estate house and killed all the cattle, but I can tell you I have a group of deputies serving search warrants down in Rails End and the Meadows area right now on several households. I think you can pretty much figure out who owns those places before tomorrow morning's Ledger hits your doorsteps. I'm hoping it's just a matter of time before we know who did it."

As Jackson walked away from the podium, Jack Jenkins and his entire family stood with a look of despair and started to walk down the front to the center aisle and leave. Three men in suits stood up from the front row of seats, along with Jennifer Thomas, and blocked their way. Doug leaned forward to the mic. "Jack Jenkins and Ron Givers, I would like to introduce you to the Owners Association's legal counsel." The men handed them some paperwork. "I would also like to introduce you to my sister, Jennifer Thomas, who's acting counsel for the Thomas, Thomas and Thomas Law Firm." Jennifer handed him some paperwork, as well. "The Owners Association and the Thomas' law firm have both just served you with papers. You're being sued, my friend, by both of us. I believe your entire family's listed on those documents."

Jack and Ron looked down at the paperwork. "Holy..." and the entire group shoved their way past the lawyers and marched to the door, throwing it open with a bang against the wall.

Jimmy and Mac watched as the group walked out to the wide mouthed stares of the audience. Jimmy quietly repeated the verse he quoted at the beginning of the morning: *"I looked, and there before me was a pale horse! Its rider was named Death, and Hell was following close behind him." –Revelation 6:8a*

Mac quietly added," Farewell, Mr. Givers. And today belongs to the Lord, the Lord Almighty—a day of vengeance, for vengeance on his foes ... and may God grant you repentance before His day is finished."

Both men looked toward Johnny, who stood with his arms crossed, staring back at them with a broad grin on his face. Grady slowly stood again, and the four men glanced at each other. The entire room watched the four men, who were the only ones standing and smiling at each other. He chuckled slightly, looking down at the floor. As they all took a seat, Valerie leaned toward him and whispered, "What was that all about? The four of you standing there and looking at each other, I mean?"

He stared at her for a long moment. "It was about Uncle Hank. It was also about the names that're carved up on that tree."

Her eyes narrowed as she stared at him. "You aren't going to explain that, are you?"

He shook his head, "No, I'm not. It's taken us forty-five years, but the Givers and Smith families are gone from Red Mill. That's all you need to know."

Doug stood up and took his place at the podium. He looked at Mac and over at Grady with a broad smile. He bounced his pen up and down lightly on the top of the podium as the silent crowd intently watched him. He leaned forward to the mic and said, "Ladies and gentlemen, as of this moment, the Red Mill Owners Association officially no longer exists. As my final public act as the president of the Red Mill Association Board, let me say, for the first time in over forty-five years, the Simmons family is again the rightful owners of Red Mill Canyon." He scanned his eyes across the quiet room, *"This meeting is adjourned!"*

As the entire room stood and started grabbing their coats, Valerie stared up at Grady. He just stood there and stared back at her for a long moment. "Go ahead and get it out, Val Gal."

She shifted in her seat as she uncomfortably stared at him. "Bill, how much of what just took place in this room did you know about beforehand? Did you plan this whole thing out?"

He leaned forward, placing a hand on both chairs on each side of her. He gently kissed her on the lips. He pulled his face back as he stared her in the eyes. "Not all of it?" Then he smiled with a huge grin. "I didn't know they were going to burn down my dad's house and kill all of the cattle. I knew they were going to do something. And you can thank Rick Seavey for catching Jared and Joey. It was his idea to put up the cameras."

She pushed him back slightly with a quaint smile. "But you knew Mac was going to offer you the land agreement for the rail line before the meeting even started, didn't you?" He remained silent and didn't say a word. "You *did* know!"

He squatted in front of her, putting his hands in her lap as he stared at her. He ran his fingers over the back of her hand in a caressing manner. "Have I ever told you you're the most beautif ..."

She jerked her hand back. "Stop it! Just answer my question!"

He chuckled slightly. He cleared his throat and said, "Mac didn't make the offer to me. I made the offer to him the day Jed and I had lunch at the Cougar and overheard them talking about the bid on the ranch. We just decided to sit on the agreement for a while just in case they did do something underhanded. We were just waiting for them to play their hand so we could catch them in the act."

She stared at him with an emotionless look. He stood and said, "You know what, let's go out on the back porch."

The two walked through the kitchen and out the back door. He took a seat on the railing and watched her fidget for a moment with her arms crossed. "I don't agree with what you just did. You led everyone in that room to think Mac was behind what just happened in that meeting, when it was actually you who orchestrated the entire thing."

He shook his head, "No, I didn't. It was Mac and Mr. Thomas, Doug's father, who planned the entire thing out. I'm just the one who made the offer to him first."

"But you knew about it, Bill, and you pretended you didn't know what was going to happen."

"Val, Mac has a saying about business. A business deal is defined by what each party thinks about the other. Sometimes you have to let them believe what you want them to believe in order to close the deal."

"That's dishonest, Bill. That's lying for personal gain."

"Only if you don't have the means to back the deal and you're trying to make them think you do! It was the other way around. We had the means to back the deal and we wanted them to think we didn't. None of us told that bunch of lowlifes to do anything wrong or break the law. We were just waiting for them to break the law because we heard them say they were going to."

She turned her head slightly, "And what if they didn't?"

He threw his hands in the air, "And what if they didn't try, forty-five years ago, to cut my grandfather out of his ownership of this place? And what if they didn't shoot Uncle Hank? Twice! And what if they didn't run a biker bar that attracts nothing but bad people to our town? And what if the Jenkins and Brines don't actually run the underground drug network in this town? Do you want me to go on about it? That's only a third of the problems those families have caused for our town. Sheriff Wilkins should have done something about it forty-five years ago."

She said, "Maybe Jimmy should have done something about it over the last ten years as Sheriff."

He intoned, "He just did, Val! And he arrested three of them last year!"

"No Grady. None of this would have happened if it wasn't for you."

"For your information, he sat on those arrests he made today because we all agreed nothing would happen until we got them to admit they were all related. That ... is what the entire goal was in there. Once Doug got them to admit they were related to Peggy Withers, Jimmy could arrest them and both groups of lawyers could serve them the papers."

She blinked a few times and asked, "How many people were involved in this?"

"It doesn't matter how many people were involved. There's only five names you need to know. The names on the tree, Val. It's about the names on the tree. We all work together. It runs way deeper than you realize."

She stared at him with a confused look. "Okay ... look. Before we get into that mysterious ... thing about the tree, which I have no clue about, apparently, I want to say one thing. Over the last few days, you lied to everyone on this ranch, making them think you couldn't back the bid. You stood right in front of that rubble that used to be Jed and Betsy house and acted all remorseful saying, *'It don't really matter. Everything I got is gone now. The Givers are just gonna bulldoze the entire town in a few days.'* Then you had Jed lead us in prayer in the hall. Betsy and Jed had their prayer time in the other bedroom in our cabin this morning. The man was crying! You made him think he lost everything. Bill, that was dishonest!"

"Was it? We talked that one out, you know. What each of us should or shouldn't say? Let me ask you this. What if I told all of you Mac and I had already made an agreement that made me two million dollars richer than everyone thought I was. And what if the Givers had someone on my payroll who was working for them and telling them what I was doing. And what about the rail yard? If they were motivated enough to burn my dad's house down, kill all of my cattle and run our trucks off a cliff, what would they have done to try to stop the Grady Corporation from agreeing to work with me on the deal? Would they have burned down the Grady Corporate offices? Maybe kidnap Mac's daughter so he wouldn't go through with the deal?"

She turned on the deck and looked off toward the trees as she thought about what he was saying. He said, "The Bible says to be gentle as lambs but wise as serpents, Val. God doesn't call us to go blindly through life and say, -*Just trust Jesus*.- That's not what the word says. And another thing. We didn't make a step without praying over all of it."

She stared off at the pine trees for a long moment and finally slid a chair at the end of the dock over in front of him. She took a seat and stared at him for a moment. "Explain the names on the tree to me."

He turned his face down to the deck for a moment. "Okay? The names on the tree were a club when I was a child."

"I know that Bill. You explained it to me last year. I want to know what the big mystery seems to be behind the five of your names. I've seen them carved on things around town. Now you're making it sound like there's a war taking place between your group and the Givers clan."

He shrugged, "I haven't heard it defined that way before, but you're not far off the mark. My family had a run in with the Givers and Smiths over forty years ago. That's why my family left Red Mill. They shot Uncle Hank. It was a feud, for lack of better words. The issue has been behind all of us for many years, but it's starting to heat up again."

"I'd say it's burning like a wildfire at the moment."

"And **that**, Val, is what that meeting was all about in the hall today. It used to be about guns. Now it's about lawyers and who has the bigger bank account. We like to do things the godly way. The Givers and Smiths? They play dirty! And believe me, it's a spiritual battle that's been tearing up Rails End for over forty years."

"What about the woman whose name's on the tree? I don't mean about the past. I mean about the *present.* What does she have to do with what just took place in the room today? Every time you talk about this you refer to the five names on the tree, not the four of you living here."

He scratched the back of his head with a grimace as he looked down at the wood planking on the dock below. "You know ... I just ..."

She waited for an answer and finally said, "Are you going to start crying on me again?"

"No! I just ... I don't know if she has anything to do with what's going on or not. I haven't heard a word about anything related to her for almost twenty-five years. Now her name has come up twice in the last month."

"With who?"

"Well, for one, Doug Thomas' father. I had a meeting with him a few weeks ago."

"The man who you just told me helped plan this out?" Grady nodded. "And he mentioned ... what's her name?"

"Cass."

"So, you were making secret plans about what just happened in that hall, and the lawyer brought up Cass in the middle of the meeting? I'd say that's more than just a coincidence."

His brow furrowed, "Val, Cass has nothing to do with our group any longer. None of us have seen her for over thirty-six years."

"You ... just told me ... it's about the five names on the tree." She stood up and crossed her arms. "Bill, you get all misty eyed whenever you talk about her. You told me not to discuss her with any of the others because it just upsets them, and now you're telling me her name has come up three times in the last month, yet she has nothing to do with you or the ranch any longer."

"Two times, not three."

She leaned toward him and intoned, **"Three times!** We're talking about her right now. That makes three. Let me ask you a question? Doug Thomas' father put this plan together and in the process of meeting with you about it, he talked about her. Did he do that to tip you off to something you didn't know about? You know nothing about her these days. Who's really pulling all the strings here? You, Ron Givers, or this Cass woman?"

He opened his mouth as if he was about to speak but just held it there, remaining silent. He looked off at the trees for a moment, his mouth still gaping open."

"You don't know the answer to that question, do you?" She studied his vacant look as he stared down at the floor below. "Don't worry. I wasn't expecting an answer."

She turned and headed to the door of the hall. Before she walked through the door, she turned back and said, "Do you want to know why I'm upset about all of this? Remember the day I gave you all those roses for your birthday?" He looked up at her with a stupid look. "I told you that day, you were buying a diamond necklace, not some cheap, costume jewelry. Do you want to know what the cost of a godly woman is? It's honesty, Bill. You said the day I was crying on the swing why you held me, we won't have any more secrets between us. No more secrets. Those were your very words. Don't treat me like a piece of costume jewelry, Bill. And the last thing I want to be treated like is a woman who has to be kept in the dark because you think I'm not smart enough or important enough to be included in decisions about our future."

She stood there, waiting for an answer. He finally lifted the front of his hat at her with his thumb and forefinger and just stared at her.

"You're such a cowboy sometimes, you know that?"

"I knew that the day you started calling me Cowboy. And about the diamond necklace thing. Have I ever told you you're the most beautiful woman in Rails End?" He slid off the railing and walked to her. "I may not know much about jewelry, but one thing I do know. You're the woman I want to marry." He put a hand under her chin and lifted it, pressing his lips against hers.

As he pulled his face back, she glared at him for a moment. She closed her eyes, drawing in a deep breath as she slowly shook her head. "Everything I just said went right over your head, didn't it?"

That evening, as the staff of the ranch met for their dinner celebration, it was anything but a party. The group had spent an hour and a half talking in the hall with all of their friends who had come to the meeting, and no one wanted to leave the room. Even Sheriff Jackson hung back as he, Mac and Rick sat and talked.

At dinner, Grady and Valerie sat quietly with the Gentrys, Rick and Mac as they talked about the events of the last two weeks. The two couples were spent. They had no energy after the two, long days. The group watched the younger crowd of staff and their families enjoying the moment as they sat around the tables at the other end of the pavilion, talking and laughing. They no longer had to fear for the future of their jobs.

During dinner, Jonathon convinced Crissy it was time to face her father. As the two walked up the road to the pavilion, one-by-one, the group sitting with Grady and Valerie simply stood and left the table to give them their space. Valerie walked out from the pavilion and hugged the tearful, young woman in the yellow, maternity dress, and led her toward the table.

Jed put his hand on Grady's shoulder. "You know how you said God was giving you a second chance to do it all over again and do it the right way? That starts right here, my friend." Jed patted him on the shoulder and walked away.

He watched her approach, and the obvious reality sank in as he looked at his daughter who was five months pregnant. And for a moment, the tension was thick in the air. He hadn't considered how the girl would look when he saw her. The moment changed everything as he eyed her vulnerability. His mind flashed back to a distant memory of his first wife, Celia, pregnant with Shawny. The girl was the splitting image of her mother. The difference was barely discernable.

Valerie lifted her head as she stared at the stunned man with a burning look, as if to say, *"Do something here. Don't just stare at her!"*

He stood and walked out to the road and touched Chrissy's face with his palm. Jonathon and Valerie walked away and left them, as he held his crying daughter in his arms. There was nothing more to be said. It was what it was and there was no denying that now.

As Jonathon took a seat at the table with the rest of the group across the pavilion, Valerie sat next to the young man and put her arm around his shoulders. The group fell silent as they ate, half of them looking down at their plates as the other half watched while the man held his crying daughter for several minutes in the center of the dirt road.

The two walked off toward the cow pasture and Valerie patted Jonathon's arm with her other hand, quoting her favorite verse from Ecclesiastes. *"There is a time for everything, and a season for every activity under the heavens." Ecclesiastes 3:1*

Jed added to what she said by quoting from the same chapter. *"He has made everything beautiful in its time. He has also set eternity in the human heart; yet no one can fathom what God has done from beginning to end."* Ecclesiastes 3:11

- 17 -

THE PINK TEDDY

The light. cooling breeze of September blew across the back lawn of the Cottage Restaurant as the four men watched from the window. They were talking in the quiet of the nearly-dark and empty dining room. Jed, Jimmy and Rick were celebrating with Grady, while they observed the ladies enjoying the wedding shower taking place on the lawn. Valerie laughed as Shawny handed her presents to open. Cynthia Spicer, the pastor's wife, was playing the perfect host, rushing about and seeing to the ladies' needs who had left the scattering of tables and were assembled in a tight group around the bride-to-be.

Jimmy nodded his head toward Missy through the window, who sat with Crissy at a table a ways from the large group of women who were cheering and chatting while Valerie unwrapped the presents. "How are things going with the youngest, Billy?"

He shook his head slightly with a look of dismay as he sat his bottle of beer on the table. "Nothins' changed much. We talk more these days, but the girl seems to be eternally pissed off. It's starting to get on my nerves, to be truthful about it. We're three days away from being hitched and she still gives Val the cold shoulder."

Rick looked out at the girl who he was so fond of. "Give it time, Bill. She'll come along. We all just need to keep praying."

He gave him a gentle smile. "I appreciate all you do for her, Rick. Going to lunch with you every week seems to make her happy. She needs the friendship you give her."

As they sat and watched, smiling at Shawny's antics while she handed the presents one at a time to Valerie, Jed looked up and asked the question everyone had been avoiding. "How's it going in Rails End, Jimmy? I understand things haven't fared so well for the Givers clan in the last few weeks."

Grady picked up his bottle and took a swig with a bitter look at Jimmy, remaining silent. The sheriff was hesitant to talk, but he finally did. "Nothing's changed about what happened out at the Acreage. I pretty much figure we caught the culprits who got their hands dirty doing it when we arrested those two in the meeting in Red Mill. As for the Jenkins, the bar and grill still looks like it did two weeks ago. The place hasn't been open since the day the townsfolk trashed it. They cleaned up the trash but more appeared this week. After that, I haven't seen hide-nor-hair of any of Jack's family."

Jimmy looked up with a slight grin on his face. "I've had several calls about it from residents. They want the Sheriff's Office to cite them for not cleaning it up again. I just figure there's no need to kick a man when he's down. Truthfully, the longer the place sits like that, with all the rotting trash in front of it, the less likely it is people will want to see the place open again. There's a reason their bar is so far off the beaten path of Mainstreet. The place was nothing but a problem for my officers on the weekends."

Jed looked up at Grady with a knowing grin which caused Jimmy to look back and forth at the two men. "What is it you're not saying here, Bill?"

Grady took another swig of his beer and looked out the window, letting Jed finish the conversation he started. "Grady told the realty office he wanted the building if it came up for sale. He got a call about it this week. Valerie's parents are buying the place. She's provided the money for it. They already signed the paperwork. Paid cash for it yesterday. They're gonna start their own café."

Jimmy loudly said, "Well thank God for that! I've spent enough nights going out there in the last five years to deal with fights!"

Jimmy continued, "Joey and Jared's little brother, Jerimiah, hightailed it out of town after the arrests. I doubt we'll ever see him again. We were told down at the office he was being the lookout on the highway when those two lit the fires. I don't have any real proof about that. I just figure he decided to get his scrawny, little butt out of Dodge once he saw his brothers being put in handcuffs. Thanking his lucky stars, that one is! Those two boys will do ten years minimum. And now I hear the Forest Service is bringing 'em up on charges at the federal level."

Grady looked up with a hateful stare, "Little Jerimiah Brine will get his in the end. You mark my word. He'll show up eventually. The kid has been as much of a problem for the town as his brothers were. Whether it's a drug deal in Sacramento or a stolen car in L.A., eventually he'll show up on the radar, and probably in someone's jail in the end."

Rick asked, "What about the Givers, Jimmy? I know they're still here. And they fixed the windows and cleaned up the graffiti."

He sat up straight in the booth seat. "The Givers are still hanging around, but they aren't doing any business right now. That office of theirs on Mainstreet has been pretty quiet. I hear Rick Maretti has been getting most of the business from the few people who are new in town and looking for a house to be built. The people talk. They tell the out-of-towners what happened. It's one thing to have a relative burn down someone's house. It's another thing entirely to kill every animal on the place and shoot an elderly man. Especially when he's already handicapped because their family shot him forty years ago."

Grady sat back and put the bottle down. "I feel sorry for those folks who did business with them out at that new housing tract. Jed and I drove by there a few days ago. They haven't replaced the sign or taken down the graffiti on the walls at the entrance. There's nothing but one, long street full of houses and a bunch of paved roads that are empty. Not a lot of value in that. The way I figure it, someone will come along and take the development over and finish what they started."

Grady and Jimmy looked out the big window and Jimmy tapped his arm from across the table with a smile. They watched as she searched for a name tag on the box she was holding. She lifted the box up high, and all the women began shaking their heads. She pulled the wrapping off the clothing store gift box, pulling a handful of pink material with lace around the edges.

The women started laughing and cheering, as Grady narrowed his eyes. She held a pink teddy to her shoulders, letting it drape down the front of her body. The entire crowd of women looked back at the window. Grady and Jimmy just stared out the window and looked at each other from the corner of their eyes. Mrs. Spicer lifted a finger and shook it at them with a knowing smile on her face. His big, bushy mustache lifted a little as the two men grinned at each other.

She put the teddy back in the box and looked at the window with a smile, blowing Grady a kiss. The ladies cheered!

As they watched her unwrap the next box, Jimmy asked, "You think she knows how to wear it?"

He was silent for a moment as he stared at her. "Doesn't have a clue!" The men at the table burst out in laughter.

"But she knows how to kiss now?"

He turned quickly, "Oh yeah! She's a fast learner once she decides to put her mind to it. It was gettin' her to do it that was the hard part." The men started laughing again.

Grady sat on the porch swing holding Valerie as he pulled her up tight to his chest, pulling her reading blanket over her body so she would be warm. "Your pa's quite the personality, Val. I love the accent. I've always taken a liking to Gaelic. What made them think about coming out this way for good?"

"Don't use the word Gaelic around him. He speaks Scottish English. There's a difference! His dad was a statesman, and you pretty much have to speak the English to talk in the U.S. I don't even understand the Gaelic. We have some relatives over from time-to-time, and they switch between the two when they talk to my daddy and don't want others to know what they're saying. He doesn't like it. He also hates it when people confuse the Scots with the Irish. Don't ever make that mistake!"

She snuggled in tighter. "My father decided to retire this year. He told me he closed his office a few months back. I'm an only child so they want to be out here now. I think this whole thing with the Givers clan has interested him. That sort of thing wouldn't happen back on the Isle of Bonnie, as my dad calls it, so he's been pretty interested in what took place up here the last few months."

She looked up at him with concern. "Grady, I want you to promise me he never finds out about what Peggy Withers pulled with that picture of me on the ledge at Sonrisa. I'm his little girl, just like Missy is yours. None of my relatives have much patience for that kind of thing. My fear is, if he ever found out, he would fly his brothers in and there would be a bloodbath the next day. They might all come from statesman lineage, but believe me, when they get mad about something, they end it decisively!"

She snuggled back in tight to him under the blanket. "He's already upset about how this thing with Jonathon and Crissy came about. My family is Scottish Presbyterian in the reformed tradition and there's no room for that kind of mistake in their mind. He sees the child as his future great-grandchild. He knows we have no plans to start a family." She looked up with a smile. "The good thing about all this is he loves the girls. He called them his granddaughters the other day. And Missy has really taken a shine to him."

"That's a good thing! The girls lost all four of their grandparents when they were kids. Celia was an only child also. The loss of their mother was the last blow for that part of their family history." After a few minutes of rocking on the swing, he said, "We serve a great God, don't we?" He looked down the path as he held her tight. "God's putting things right, Val Gal."

The two watched through the trees toward the buildings near the front gate as a white SUV pulled up to the security shack. He lifted his arm from her shoulder. "That's Mac's Suburban. He's probably here to see me. We need to talk about the cabin I plan to give him up here."

He stepped off the porch as the vehicle pulled up in front of his cabin. Mac stepped out and shook his hand, holding a legal envelope. "Valerie," he said with a nod of his head.

"Plan to stay for dinner?" she asked as she sat up, crossing her legs with an arm across the back of the seat where Grady had been sitting.

"No. My daughter's cooking ours right now. Maybe next time." He looked at Bill and said, "We need to talk."

"About the cabin?"

"That too." The two men walked up the hill toward the church and took a seat on a bench halfway up the path. He cleared his voice and said, "About the cabin. I appreciate the offer, Billy. I'd like to keep the one I use near the big Lodgehouse on Owners Row. I paid a lot of money to fix it up the way I wanted it about five years ago. The board agreed to that. If Donny and Jed are okay with it, that's the one I want."

"Done! I have no problem with that. Everyone up here knows you've used the cabin for years when you come up. Is that it?"

He scooted sideways a bit and laid his hand across the back of the bench seat. "We might have a problem."

"Define we?"

"The names on the tree."

Grady said, "The Mulligans?" grinning at him.

His head jolted up, looking at him. "Where did you dig that name out of? I haven't heard that name in thirty-five years."

"Hank called us that a few weeks ago. Is the problem with the Givers?"

"No." He pulled a letter and a photo from the envelope, handing the letter to him. "It's a letter from *Five Star Corporation* cancelling the debt on my house. I took a second out on my house a few years ago to teach my daughter about credit and how to manage loans. We used the money to remodel my office and her bedroom. It was just a few thousand dollars, but it was a way of teaching her about setting up loans and launching out on her own to build credit."

"Why did you go to Ron Givers for a loan?"

"It was a local company. I keep my money inside the town. Ron offered lower amounts for a second on the mortgage."

"Why would he cancel the debt?"

"He didn't, Billy. He sold the company three months ago because he was trying to defer debt in order to purchase Red Mill. Exactly thirty days after the sale, an investment company purchased Five Star from the new owner. The new company who owns it wrote off my debt. They also wrote off the debt Drake at the hardware store owed them and it was a $30,000 balance."

"You know, I heard the Givers and the Jenkins talking about this at the Cougar in that meeting I told you about. Okay, a little stupid but good news for you and Drake. I'm assuming there's some bad news coming here?"

Mac stared at him for a moment and finally asked, "Have you ever sold a company before?"

"No. I've sold a lot of cattle and a few properties. Never a company."

"When you buy a company as the new owner, all contracts are void and have to be renegotiated, *if*, the new owner demands it. It doesn't always happen, but the new owner can force a renegotiation or simply terminate agreements. Ron Givers sold *Five Star* and managed to pile all of his corporate debts on the balance of the books as part of the deal, in order to defer payments on those debts for thirty years. It was $300,000 dollars. Four weeks later, a company called *Firm Fund Fifty-Five* purchased the company from the new owner and gave Ron Givers a letter of demand and foreclosed on the entire $300,000 he'd been trying to defer. It happened to him three days before he put his bid in on the purchase of Red Mill."

Mac pulled a second letter out of his envelope and handed it to Grady. "This is a letter *Firm Fund Fifty-Five* sent to Doug Thomas making him aware, as the head of the committee selling Red Mill, they had just called in a $300,000 marker on a debt owed by Givers Development Company."

Grady said, "That's a little odd. How did they know he was even bidding on Red Mill?"

"Exactly. Odd, but it's not illegal to protect your interests by letting another organization know a debt's owed to you, if you think they might spend the money they owe to you on some other investment."

"Okay," Grady said, "So God handed us a nice push when the bids went in." Mac just stared at him but didn't say a word. "Didn't he?"

He slowly shook his head. "It wasn't God who did it. I did some investigation into Firm Fund Fifty-Five. It's owned by a trust which was set up in Iowa twenty-five years ago. The term Fifty-Five means five funds in five different states. When you set up an investment pool, you spread your money over twenty sources of investment. It's called the *rule of risk averages* in finance terms. They teach this when you take finance in college. The reason you do that is to spread your risk out over all areas possible. After you hit twenty investments, you start duplicating efforts. Twenty's the key number. This company chose twenty-five, but it still follows pretty closely to the *rule of risk averages* on investments."

"Mac ... I'm assuming you have a good reason for putting me through a finance course here. Just tell me why you're so concerned."

"Before my father died, he put a lot of our corporate stock into a trust for old friends who he wanted to thank someday. He made regular disbursements of stock into the account for many years. As he got older, I was the one who managed the disbursements for him. One third of the Grady Corporation's privately owned voting stock is in that trust. Now, I happened to know that ... that Cass ... and her mother were one of the people who benefited from that trust. It was to help them after what happened forty years ago. Firm Fund Fifty-Five is owned by that very same trust in Iowa. This can't be a coincidence, Bill. Apparently, the stock trust my father set up, either purchased ... or started Firm Fund Fifty-Five."

Grady furrowed his brow deeply. Mac said, "Here's what I'm really worried about." He handed him an eight by ten photo of five people standing in an office. "I pulled this off the internet. Firm Fund has a website." He breathed in heavily and stated, "When my father died, I was given responsibility for anything relating to Cass. She used to be my girlfriend when we were kids. You know that. I've visited her twice since my father's death. The woman in the middle with the blonde hair? It's Cass, Billy."

After he studied her picture, Mac said, "She runs Firm Fund Fifty-Five. It's owned by my dad's trust, which she's one of the beneficiaries of. The trust is a blind trust. Only the recipients of the trust can get any information about it. She purchased Five Star Loan Agency and just used it to meddle in the sale of Red Mill to make it easier for you or old man Drake to win the bid. Not only that, but when Ron Givers tried to knock his $300,000 dollar corporate debt off, to improve his position when he sold Five Star, she bought the company who owned the debt and spiked it back in his face like she was spiking a volley ball back over a net at him."

Grady asked, "You're sure about this? That it's not a coincidence?"

"Bill, she followed the rule of twenty when she started Firm Fund. The five extra investments are all in Rails End. The fund has interests in Rails End Bank, the bank in Temple Ridge, the Cattle Lands Coop and Trust Association and now the Five Star Corporation. Her bank investments give her the ability, as a stockholder, to review all of our finances. The Givers, Drake, your accounts, and even a lot of my own finances. She knew exactly where each of you stood, financially, who bid on the property. The fifth investment is a land speculation deal which just happens to be a piece of land I was trying to purchase as a backup just in case the deal between you and I fell through on the rail line. I got in a bidding war over the property with Firm Fund Fifty-Five. She stopped me from purchasing the property. She won the bid."

"Mac, that makes no sense. Only cattle ranchers would want that property, other than you."

"Billy, she purposely cut me out of the deal to make sure you would be the only direction I could go with the new rail line. She did it to purposely set this up so that you would have the money you needed to buy Red Mill. Then she foreclosed the debt on the Givers, which dropped them down to par with Drake when he bid. She cancelled Drake's debt in order to bring his portfolio up to par with the Givers. Do you know what the other bids came in at? Drake was a thousand dollars lower than the Givers on the bid. She almost succeeded in making him the backup bid when they burned your dad's house and killed all the cattle. If Drake had bid just a thousand and one dollars higher, the sale would have reverted to him if you couldn't close the deal. And I have no doubt in my mind that if Drake had won the bid, he probably would have sold part of Red Mill to you to do whatever you want with it. He was just looking for a retirement property. He's too old to be serious about starting a new venture."

Grady sat back on the bench and looked down the road toward his cabin. "You know what Val asked me after that meeting. She asked me who was really pulling all the strings? Us, the Givers or Cass? Apparently, Cass still has a heart for the town and the club."

Mac said, "Well she definitely didn't want the Givers to take over Red Mill, which tells me the names on that tree up there on the rim still holds the same meaning it did in the past, in her mind, as much as it does in ours."

Grady said, "Don't discuss this with Jimmy or Johnny! Just let her play out her hand in the future so we can figure out what she's doing and why."

- 18 -

THE WOMAN IN WHITE

The following Saturday, an entire row of tables was packed at the Roadhouse Restaurant as the group celebrated the final meal, a tradition Valerie's family insisted on. "Different families have different traditions," she told Grady, "And it would be a dress up affair." He walked in wearing his dark, cowboy suit and tails with his newer black, felt hat on. The cowboys had all agreed earlier in the morning. If the Scots would have their kilts and white shirts on, adorned with the large, matching ties which hung past their waists, and black coats adorned with sporran at the cuffs, then the cowboys would wear their dress hats and collarless, linen shirts, complete with sliver and turquoise buttons which snapped up the front.

While the group from the ranch stood inside the door, Greggory Dobbins introduced his brothers Gilchrist and Gillanders. Both men wore the traditional, Scottish-green kilt and long, wide tie. He stood in the red kilt and tie which was reserved for the place of honor they gave him, as the father of the bride.

The cowboys stared down at the men's stockings and Ghillie brogues, and the Scottish looked down at their fancy, leather boots all polished to a luster. Grady and Greggory looked up, and the two men laughed as her father gave him a hearty slap on the back. "I guess we're not so different after all, now are we, son?"

The packed room looked on with snickers and snorts as the two groups took their places at the table to order breakfast. When Valerie entered in the dress her mother had sown for her, the room fell silent. Her father stood to look on his daughter, who wore a green overlay of vest and runners, over a white dress with long, baggy sleeves. The whole group stood with him as she took her place of honor next to her groom at the table.

Patrick continued to stand as the group sat, and announced in a Scottish brogue, "Well aren't we an odd assortment. The look-a-the-town, I suppose." When the ordering was finished and the plates were served, the waitress gave him the bill.

After a hour of fanfare and eating, Valerie watched with a smile, holding onto Grady's arm, as her father chatted with Shawny, Missy and Crissy. *"They really are infatuated with my father,"* she whispered into his ear as they watched the group at the other end of the table. *"He knows how to treat the ladies, Cowboy!"* she smiled.

As the two looked on, Greggory became quiet and listened to the girls. The celebration of the moment began to turn. Valerie let go of his arm, and he looked at her with concern, as she watched her father. "What's the matter, Val?" he said as she suddenly sat straight. She watched as the group of Scottish men became agitated.

She looked at Grady with a fear in her eyes. "Something's wrong, Bill. This isn't good!" Shawny stared down the long row of tables at the two, with a look of panic. As the discussion became more animated, Greggory leaned forward toward Gilchrist and Gillanders with a look of righteous anger.

She whispered under her breath *"No ... no, no, no, Daddy! Not today, please! Not on my wedding day!"* Grady looked at her, and back at the men who sat with his daughters. They watched while Greggory grilled Missy with a burning fire in his eyes. The other two girls looked their way in wide-eyed shock.

She jumped from her seat, but it was too late. The three Scotsmen stood and headed for the door. Valerie turned back and yelled, **"She told him about the photo, Grady! The picture of me at Sonrisa!"**

Grady stood to rush for the door after the Scots walked out. He turned back unsure what to do as Valerie ran across the hall in a panic. He called to Jed and the boys, **"Get up and get out here with me, now!"**

The entire group of cowboys jumped from their seats and followed their boss out the door. The group assembled on the sidewalk, followed by the entire room of diners, watching the three men march down the center of Mainstreet. Valerie chased after them, her green draping flying in the air. The three Scots headed toward the Givers Development office, removing their coats and ties, dropping them in the middle of the road. They were marching faster now with six, clenched fists.

Jed looked up at his boss, "What do we do?"

Grady removed his own coat. "We're gonna do what we should have done a year ago, boys!" He threw his coat and hat on the cement walkway, heading off toward the three Scots at a quick pace. The cowboys followed his lead, stripping their coats and hats off and marching after him like a pack of wolves who were ready for a fight.

She pleaded with her father as she caught up to him, but he brushed his daughter off. **"Stay out of the way, little girl!"** he yelled. As she turned to look at Grady, the gang of cowboys following, she stood there with her hands to her mouth. He had a hardened look as they marched past her with the crowd of a hundred town folk following to watch what was about to happen.

"Grady … Grady, no! Please don't do this!" She leaned forward shaking her fists as she yelled, **"It's our wedding day, Grady!"** But her pleading was useless. The Scots were ready to set things right and he wasn't about to let them try to do it alone. As the group of women from the wedding party caught up with her, the ladies huddled in front of the crowd, standing in Mainstreet. Her father threw the door of the Givers Development office open with a glass shattering bang. She waved her fists in the air with a frustrated look and collapsed into a pile of white and green fluff and fury, sitting on the asphalt with the ladies surrounding her.

Ron Givers had a room full of construction workers assembled in the office, explaining that the company was closing. As the man was standing before his employees, along with his uncle Jack, the entire group stood when the door crashed open. The three Scots marched through the center of the seats, pushing men aside.

And the fight was on!

They grabbed Ron and Jack, running them across the room toward the big, plate glass window which looked toward Mainstreet.

Five bodies were moving rapidly across the room toward the window and the cowboys stood on the sidewalk waiting for them. The two men came flying through the newly installed, plate glass window, landing on the cement outside with a shower of glass raining down everywhere. The bride-to-be wrapped her arms over her head and sunk toward her lap. Ron and Jack struggled to stand, somewhat dazed as they tried to make sense of who these garish men were. Grady grabbed Jack and hit him hard with a punch to the face, sending the man backwards through the window again as he fell over the foot-high, wood retainer of the missing window. Valerie rolled her eyes dramatically and yelled, **"Bill Simmons!"** with a look of anger, but he ignored her as the group of cowboys jumped through the window to help the three Scots, who had been pulled into the crowd of brawny, construction workers with dozens of flying fists.

Ron was on his feet again. As he tried to leap through the window, old Jed hit him with a hard left to the face and the man fell back to the sidewalk again like a spiked volleyball that didn't make it over the net. Seconds later, Jed himself came flying through the window, taking a hard punch from a burly, construction worker. Valerie and Betsy ran to the man, who was too old to be fighting this kind of fight, and they drug him from the sidewalk to the asphalt. Betsy sat on him, yelling, **"Stay put, Jed!"**

The room was being torn to pieces as chairs took flight and fists flew. The brawling crowd, one-by-one, came flying or jumping out of the window. The group in the street backed up a ways, giving the brawlers a wide berth. The street in front of the Givers office was a blurry montage of flying arms and fists. The pavement was full of cowboys, flying kilts and construction workers, in the biggest brawl to ever take place in the small town of Rails End.

The crowd ran to the other side of the street as police cruisers screamed down Mainstreet from all directions and came to a halt, doors flying open and uniforms plunging into the chaos of fists. The officers tried to break up the fight, and the scene became a flurry of fists and nightsticks. The command vehicle came to a halt and Sheriff Jackson threw his door open. He watched his deputies beating the angry mob, trying to stop the fight. He noticed as a knife was brandished, and pulled the Glock 9mm pistol from his holster. He pointed it straight up in the air, firing three rounds with an ear-splitting noise which seized everyone's attention. Most of the men fell to the pavement. The fight stopped dead in its tracks. **"Everyone on the sidewalk, now!"**

The officers pushed the men back ordering them to sit on the curb. As the group of men in torn and blood-stained clothing took a spot on the curb, the sheriff spoke with his deputies in a huddle. After a few minutes the Sheriff walked to the end of the crowd and paced the full length of the group, looking the men over. He stopped as he stared at his best friend and slowly shook his head. "Seriously?" Grady lifted both hands from his lap with a slight shrug.

And that's when the embarrassing finale occurred!

It was more than Valerie could bear. The town folk watched as the Reverend and Mrs. Spicer slowly drove down Mainstreet in their car, their mouths gaping open, completely unaware of what had taken place. It was the only vehicle moving, on what was normally the busiest day of the week. He and his wife were leaving town to head up the hill to the ranch to get ready for the wedding. As they slowly drove by, looking at the huge crowd on one side of the street, and the line of bloodied men on the other, he stopped his car right in the middle of the road. The parson got out and stood there, looking at his entire wedding party sitting on the curb, full of cuts and bruises, trying to make sense of the entire scene.

Reverend Spicer walked closer to the group of men sitting on the curb, a mess of torn suits, kilts and jeans, and it was then that he realized Grady was sitting right in the middle of the bunch. Blood was running down his face and dripping on his Sunday shirt, which had a growing pattern of red spreading across his chest as the shirt absorbed the color. Don held his hands in the air and yelled in shock, **"Bill?"**

Valerie cringed and turned away, staring at Betsy, who stood behind her with tightly pressed lips. She could see Valerie's face turning bright red as she clenched her fists tight. Betsy closed her own eyes and quickly shook her head from side-to-side. Valerie turned and marched across Mainstreet in all the regalia of her traditional, Scottish dress, the green furls blowing in the wind while most of the town watched. She marched past Don and approached her tall groom with a fire in her eyes. She yelled, **"Stand up, Bill Simmons!"**

He complied, struggling a bit as he stood to walk toward her. She pulled on the right sleeve of her dress, hiking it up her arm. She reared her fist back as he was leaning forward and punched him with a hard right hook across his jaw. Grady fell backward as his feet hit the curb, laying him out on the sidewalk.

Betsy cringed hard with her shoulders raised, tightly closing her eyes. The entire crowd let out a collective sound of shock that reverberated down Mainstreet.

She lifted both sides of her white dress and marched quickly down the row of men to her father, who was sitting between both of her uncles. She stood there and glared at him for a moment. She lifted her arm slightly with a clenched fist. Gilchrist and Gillanders, both, leaned away from Gregory with a shrinking look, as he closed his eyes, waiting for the punch. Tears filled her eyes and she yelled, **"Why Daddy? It's been ten years! Why did it have to be on my wedding day?"**

The angry bride turned with a flurry of green draping on white, lifting both sides of the long dress as she marched off down the center of Mainstreet, a parade of one. Valerie Dobbins, the town surgeon and bride to be, was the sole winner of the brawl! The town looked on in complete silence. Nothing but the blowing wind and the flapping of green material could be heard, which flew in the air like a cape behind her body as she stormed down the middle of Mainstreet.

Three o'clock that afternoon, the organ music echoed across the Meadow in all directions. The bride-to-be walked slowly through the red, Russian grass on a white runner which was lined with flowers on both sides.

The afternoon had been a flurry of work as Betsy and Mrs. Dobbins repaired the three Scottish kilts, cleaning them so Greggory, Gilchrist and Gillanders would be ready for the ceremony.

As she slowly walked down the runner, she met her father, smiling at the man with the red welt on his face. He took her arm and led her between the rows of seated guests. Shawny and Crissy were all aglow as their pretty, lavender dresses shimmered in the sunlight.

Grady, Rick and Jed watched her approach, standing in their tuxes, Grady in white and the others in black, with a cummerbund of lavender for each. The groom tried to smile with a swollen lip and a bright-red cut on his face. Reverend Spicer struggled to keep from laughing at the display of men who stood and sat before him. Gilchrist had a black eye and Gillanders had two bruises on his face, sitting on the left side of the front row. He looked to the right side where Jonathon sat with his arm in a sling, a part of the Simmons family now. Behind him sat Donavan and Jason with bruises and cuts on their faces. Never had he seen such a sight at a wedding in his twenty years of officiating these kinds of gatherings. Never had he seen such a sight like what he drove up on in Rails End earlier that morning.

The ceremony came to the time of the vows, and he asked, "Do you, Bill Simmons, take this woman, to be your wife, to have and to hold from this day forward, for better or for worse, for richer, for poorer, in sickness and in health, to love and to cherish, until death do you part?"

Grady looked at him and stated, "I do!"

He turned to Valerie and asked, "Do you, Valerie Dobbins, take this man, to be your husband, to have and to hold from this day forward, for better or for worse, for richer, for poorer, in sickness and in health, to love and to cherish, until death do you part?"

She stared at her tall groom with the beaten-up face and remained silent. After a long hesitation, the pastor said in a quiet tone, "*Valerie?*"

She looked toward the pastor and loudly replied, **"I'm thinking here, Don!"** She turned her head back and stared at Grady with an angry look, to the chuckles of the audience. She said, "I guess so!" with a cock of her head and forced smile.

He announced, "I now pronounce you man and wife."

She reached up and ran her finger over the bulge in his lip with a pouting look and kissed him. She pulled her lips back and rubbed his swollen lip again. She suddenly pushed hard on it with a twist of her thumb. Grady jerked his head back with a wounded look of pain. She whispered, *"You're such an idiot!"* giving him a quiet, angry stare. Reverend Spicer snorted out a grin, trying hard not to laugh.

Mac sat with the groom at the pavilion table and chatted with him after the reception. The men on the ranch cleaned the pavilion and folded up the extra tables. Grady looked up at him with a quiet demeanor, "Thank you, Mac. I'll never be able to pay you back for what you did for me by backing my bid for this place."

He smiled back softly, "Just call it your wedding present. We took an oath many years ago, right?"

Grady's eyes slowly lowered and stared at the metal table. "That was a long time ago, my friend. But yes, we did and it's probably best not to talk about it. Jimmy and Johnny are still on the property. It really has no meaning anyway, after Cass left."

He slowly drew an envelope out of his pocket and slid it across the table to him. "This is for you. It's probably best you throw it away after you read it."

Grady looked up and his brow furrowed as he watched the tears begin to well up in Mac's eyes. He breathed in hard, looking back down at the table. "I shouldn't have mentioned her name. It wasn't your fault, Mac. None of us are responsible for what happened. We had no control over what our parents did."

He looked off across the meadow. He struggled to hold his emotions back as the tears began to stream down his cheeks.

"Mac … this is why we agreed to never talk about her again! That idiot lawyer in Los Angeles dredged up the past and threw it back in our lap. What does Cass have to do with the ranch and the Thomas law firm?"

He wiped the tears away with his hand and looked at his old friend. "Aside from helping you win the bid on the ranch, she really has nothing to do with it. My dad had Doug Sr. handle some stuff to help her and her mother out after the trial. That's all. He shouldn't have even brought it up."

"Then why are you sitting here blubbering about this. It's been thirty-six years. That's long enough to get over a childhood girlfriend and everything that happened."

He moved his eyes toward the card on the table with a nod of his chin. "Just read the card!"

Grady lifted the envelope and opened it, pulling a wedding card out.

"Congratulations, Billy! God giveth and God taketh away. Today, it's the other way around. I want you to know all four of you have always been dear to my heart. I'm so sorry for the past and everything that happened. I'm doing well and God has blessed me greatly. Maybe someday we'll be able to see each other again. I completely understand if you don't want to, but it would make my heart glad if we did. Mac talked to me about Firm Fund Fifty-Five and my purchasing the Five Star Corporation. He told me you know about it. Making sure you won the bid was your wedding present from me. Go and live your grandfather's dream."

Winnie Cassmore

Cass

Grady just sat there staring at the card. He slowly shook his head from side-to-side. He looked up at Mac with tears in his own eyes. His breathing began to shudder, and he started crying. Mac reached out across the table and took his hand, holding it as they both cried.

Grady intoned loudly, **"Why? That's what I'd like to know. It makes no sense! Why did he do it?"** He looked away as he cried for a moment. **"He destroyed her life and ours along with it! Every one of the families suffered because of what he did!"**

Mac took a napkin that was laying on the table, wiping his eyes and blowing his nose. "I don't want to sit here and rehash conversations we had no answers to twenty-five years ago. We agreed to just walk away from this and leave it in the past. And he didn't destroy our families. Well … not yours and mine, anyway."

Grady blurted out, "Jimmy and Johnny's! And Cass'! My family completely changed after we took in Jimmy and Johnny. Not that I don't value them as a brother, but my family was different after what that man did to us." He raised his palms in the air and said, "You right. We don't need to go over all of this again. This is supposed to be one the happiest nights of my life."

"Keep the card just between us, Billy. My dad told me to never discuss what's going on with Cass, but if she reached out, then let her do it. To my knowledge, you're the first person from Rails End who she's ever contacted. I doubt you'll ever hear anything from her again, so cherish this moment, but don't discuss it with anyone."

He handed the card back to Mac, who tore it pieces, tossing it in the trash can next to the table.

Grady headed back to his cabin, looking for Valerie as he

watched Mac drive off, unsure where she had disappeared to. The last he had seen of her, she was walking arm-in-arm with Shawny up the dirt road along the cow pasture while the last of the cars pulled out of the ranch. He called out to Donavan who was walking toward the office. "Donny, make sure the cabins we made up for the Scots are ready. I left three bottles of Wild Turkey on my desk in the office. Let 'em know what a good, American whiskey tastes like. They earned it today!" he said with a laugh.

Shawny approached her father, who was heading down the cabin path aside the meadow, and gave him a big hug. "I love you, Daddy. *Have a good niiiight*!" she said in a coy voice.

"Where's Valerie? I've been looking for her for a half-hour."

She raised her eyebrows with a smile and turned backwards as she passed her father, her hands behind her back. She did a small sashay from side-to-side, dancing slightly. "You know how you said to Val that she's the most beautiful woman in Rails End?"

He cleared his voice, "I don't know I want to answer that question right before ..." He gave a small laugh with an embarrassed look. "I don't want to talk about this!"

"Exactly!" she admonished. "And if I ever hear you complain about Valerie the way you complained about mom in the past?" She pointed at him and said, "God has given you a second chance. And don't forget this night in the future. Rarely does a man get to visit his youth again, thirty years later." She stepped up to him and gave him a quick kiss on the lips. "Don't mess this up, Papa. If I have a say in it, this is the woman who I'd want for a stepmother. Don't mess this up!"

She turned and departed in silence. He stood there and smiled as he watched his oldest daughter hike down the side of the meadow. He turned and continued down the path to the back of his cabin, walking around to the front yard. As he stepped up on the porch, he put his hands on his hips, staring at Crissy, who was laying on the swinging love seat on her side, her head perched on Valerie's folded porch blanket.

He walked over and sat on the wood slats in front of her with his hands behind his body to prop himself up. "I hope you're not planning to sit on my porch all night. The call of the wild and all that."

"Eeeuw, Daddy. That's just gross!"

He chuckled lightly. "You're the only daughter I can make those kinds of jokes with, now that you're having a baby."

She darted her eyes away in shame and he inched his body closer to her and held her hand. "It's time to accept it and move on. That means we can joke about it." He watched her for a moment and asked, "What were you thinking about?"

She took the end of the blanket and held it up to her nose. "I was thinking her blanket smells like her." She watched his silent attitude for a moment and said, "She's a good woman, Daddy. She's done a lot to help Jonathon and me in the last year. I really like her! Do you want me to tell you a little secret?"

He shrugged and said, "As long as you don't expect me to tell you one back?"

"I have trouble sleeping lately. I'm getting bigger. Sometimes I come out here on your porch in the middle of the night and sleep on this swing." After a long, quiet moment she said, "I like the smell of her blanket. It reminds me of her. It helps me sleep."

"Whatever gets you through it. Just between you and me, I like the way she smells, also."

"Then you're gonna like tonight!" She smiled, looking down at the wood slats of the porch. They both were quiet for a minute as they enjoyed the cool of the evening. "What was Mom's and your wedding like?"

He turned his head and gave her a stupid smile but remained silent for twenty seconds. She stared at him with a probing look. He said, "You really want to do this? On my wedding night?" He looked away briefly. He sat up and took her hand again. "It was beautiful! We had a wedding out on the acreage, just like today. Half the town came to the wedding. My family ran with all the well-known families in town. Grandpa goes all the way back to the start of the timber operation up here. He and your great grandfather helped establish rails end." He lifted his hands in the air and said, "It was a royal wedding for Rails End. It was exactly what your momma wanted. She was very happy that day."

He watched as she struggled, as if she were about to cry. "What color was your wedding?"

"I ... don't remember. You'd have to look at the photo book and see."

Crissy stared at him, her eyes blinking away the tears. She suddenly burst out with a loud wail turning her face to the blanket to muffle her crying. Her voice shuddered as she said, "I couldn't remember what mom looked like the other day. I went into your cabin and looked at the photos in the guest room. You took her framed photo off the wall."

He slowly nodded his head. "The way I figure it, my house belonged to the memories of both of us up until the moment I was engaged. Now it belongs to Val. She doesn't need to be looking at photos of the woman she replaced and wondering what mine and your mom's life was like."

As the tears streamed from her eyes, he held his hand to his daughter's face. "You're struggling with this aren't you. Me getting married again. It's like your mother never existed."

She lifted her head slightly, shaking it. "No. I like Valerie. I think she's a wonderful person!" She sat up on the swing seat, wiping her face with both hands as she sniffled loudly. He took the hanky Val had given him from his pocket and handed it to her, watching her blow her nose. She struggled with a quivering face as she looked at her father. "I feel guilty!"

"Why?"

She held the hanky in the air with her mouth open, trying hard to find the right words. She sighed heavily and stated, "Because I like Valerie so much. She's ..." her eyes filled with tears again and she couldn't say it.

He said, "If you had your choice, you'd rather be with Valerie?"

"Yes! ... Yes! I'm not supposed to feel that way about my real mother. When I was a kid, Mom would take me to a store and grab me by the arm and drag me around with her. If we were shopping for clothes, she didn't *ask* me what I wanted. She *told* me what I wanted. Sometimes I would just want a pair of jeans and she would dress me up like something I didn't want to be. It was about what she wanted, not about what I needed."

He breathed in a long breath, "Yep! There was a lot of that going on. Me too. It's my fault, Crissy. I should have stepped in when you were young and redirected the issue. I failed to do that. I'm sorry." He stroked the back of her hand with his big thumb.

"Did you know Valerie drove to Lamont a few weeks before we came home?"

He raised his eyebrows. "No. I didn't."

"She took me shopping. We went to a maternity store. When I asked her what I should buy, you know what she said? She told me to buy whatever I want. Just pick out seven dresses to wear that I like. Then she told me I was raised to do what mama told me to do. Now it was time to start thinking for myself. Then she sat there and actually talked with me about the dresses. For the first time I had a fun time shopping for clothes."

"And now you're feeling guilty because you enjoy shopping with Valerie, and you didn't with Mom?"

She turned her head with a slight whine in her voice. "Noooo? I'm feeling guilty because I like Valerie better than I do Mom. I feel bad about that. The other day I caught myself thinking I wished Valerie would have just been our mother from the beginning."

He stood and pulled on her hand, standing her up. He held her in his arms. "I guess a man can't ask for more from his daughter than that, on the day he marries his new wife. And speaking of new wife, where is she?"

She stared at him with a slight grin, wiping the wetness from her cheeks. She gave him a kiss and said, "I'm sure she'll be along soon enough." As she stepped from the porch to the lawn she said, "Pretty in pink, Daddy!" She smiled, "Beautiful is a better word."

He just stared at her for a moment, "Ya' know, I dodged that conversation with your sister up the trail a ways and I ain't about to have it with you, either."

"Oh! I see!" she said as she nodded. "The call of the wild and all that!"

He lifted his hands to his chest and started beating them.

"Don't do that when your alone with Val! You look really stupid." She turned and walked away.

He walked into the cabin and shut the heavy, wooden door. He pulled everything from his pockets, throwing his car keys and wallet on the dining room table and went into the bathroom to take a shower. After he showered, he entered the hallway and threw the door to his bedroom open, drying off with the towel. The half-dark room flickered with candlelight.

The groom stood in the doorway with a look of surprise, surveying the room which had been decorated by Crissy and Shawny. He peered in to see Valerie on the comforter of the bed, propped up on her elbows, wearing the pink teddy. As he stood in shock, she watched him with a solid stare for a moment. She said, *"Pursue me, Bill Simmons!"*

Grady and Valerie hid in the peacefulness of their small, cabin room. The room that, from this night forward, would be theirs to share. A young woman sat in the darkness of the pavilion which still hung with streamers from the reception. She shivered in the dark, night air as she pulled her ugly, black jacket over the pretty, lavender dress she had bitterly agreed to wear to the wedding.

Missy leaned forward on her knees, in a cowgirl manner, all alone and missing her mother. Everything had changed! The father she had loved was a man she no longer knew. Her dead mother had been replaced. She now hated Red Mill Canyon and its memories of the past!

Her face soured and started to quiver. She pulled the coat shut tightly to her body and began to rock gently as her body shook.

Although no one could hear it, the loud moaning of a lonely, young woman pierced the darkness of the meadow. In that bitter moment, Missy Simmons came to a resolve. She was done with going to college and wanted no part of this new, family arrangement … *and she had no intentions of letting Valerie Dobbins take her mother's place!*

NOTE TO READER: If you liked this book, please take time to review it on Amazon.com. Your reviews make authors successful. Thanks!

LOVE COMES LATELY: BOOK 1

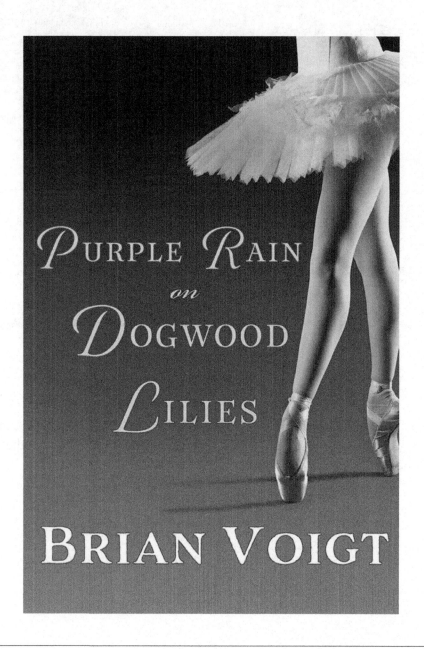

$\mathcal{P}$URPLE $\mathcal{R}$AIN

ON

$\mathcal{D}$OGWOOD

$\mathcal{L}$ILIES

Buckley Yates, a federal investigator, arrives for his new assignment in Markleeville, California. What awaits him is a storm in the making, as he discovers that Sarah Scullings, a bad omen from his past, is living in the tiny town of 300 residents. The lovely ballerina and business owner turns his life and investigation into turmoil while he learns that, in a town of 300 people, there is no way to avoid each other. Two souls begin to be drawn together, as Sarah runs from her past, while Buck is trying to run from her. Every step in opposite directions pulls them closer and closer together till the truth of a long misunderstanding, explodes into a love affair that they both have spent eighteen years running from. "Purple Rain on Dogwood Lilies" is about a terrorist investigation for the Department of Homeland Security which occurs in Monitor Pass, California, and a healing of two souls who both love, hate and have avoided each other for years.

Love comes Lately: Book 2

RED HAIL FALLING is the conclusion of *Purple Rain on Dogwood Lilies*, a suspenseful ride of romance, and a power struggle between the CIA and the Russian Mafia, for control of the Eastern Sierra communities. Charger Team races, under Sawyer Manning's leadership, to close a loophole in their previous investigation that now has Buck, Sarah and Sawyer as the ones being hunted.

RED HAIL FALLING offers a piercing look into the soul of an interracial relationship between two people who have both been married previously and come from very different families and lifestyles. As Sawyer experiences the worst three days of his life, it leaves him struggling with how to manage his embattled team of investigators, approach a relationship with Sally Jones that is becoming serious, and understand the conflicts of growing up in South Atlanta as he dates a woman that is from one of the wealthiest families in the Eastern Sierras.

Buck and Sarah Yates settle in Red Mill Canyon as they grapple with the onset of a disease that takes an unexpected turn. They are left perplexed as to what God is doing in their life, as Buck learns the depth of why Sarah spent ten years of her life immersed in an investigation for the CIA and the importance it held for several U.S. intelligence agencies, as they are both drawn back into an investigation that the couple had hoped they could move on from.

ABOUT THE AUTHOR

Brian Voigt is a writer and novelist who is local to the Midwest heartlands. He lives in the Iowa farming country with his wife. Brian holds a bachelor's degree in business and has over thirty years of experience in newspaper marketing and management, having worked for distinguished news organizations including the Arizona Republic, Phoenix New Times, New Times Los Angeles and Gatehouse Media during his career, as well as running Voigt News

Services. He also has fifteen years of experience working in non-profit ministry with children and community services. As a writer, he worked in Central Arizona as a newspaper publisher, news writer and opinion columnist. He's also been published in Smithsonian Magazine concerning life in the Sierra High Desert region. His books are Christian western romance and investigative mystery, with an emphasis on family life and healing relationships. Brian has authored *Purple Rain on Dogwood Lilies*, *Red Hail Falling*, and the *Red Mill Canyon* series, the first three of which, *Winters Edge*, *Refiners Fire* and *Autumns Child* have already been published, with four additional books waiting to go to press.

Made in the USA
Middletown, DE
13 April 2022

64174523R00106